The Face . . .

The player started to dribble. Lost the ball. I saw the angry scowl on his face.

His face.

No!

He had the face—the face in my drawing!

"It's him!" I shrieked, grabbing for Adriana. "It's him! It's him!"

Another Shadyside player turned. He had the face too!

I stared at two more players.

Stared at their wavy brown hair. Their turned-up noses. Their serious, dark eyes.

They all had the face I'd been drawing.

The face of the dead boy.

And as they turned to stare back at me, their smiles faded. Their mouths twisted. Eyes bulged in horror.

They all started to scream.

And I screamed with them.

Books by R. L. Stine

Available from ARCHWAY Paperbacks

FEAR STREET®
R·L·STINE

TheFace

A Parachute Press Book

AN ARCHWAY PAPERBACK
Published by POCKET BOOKS
New York   London   Toronto   Sydney   Tokyo   Singapore

This book is a work of fiction. Names, characters, places and incidents are products of the author's imagination or are used fictitiously. Any resemblance to actual events or locales or persons, living or dead, is entirely coincidental.

AN ARCHWAY PAPERBACK *Original*

An Archway Paperback published by
POCKET BOOKS, a division of Simon & Schuster Inc.
1230 Avenue of the Americas, New York, NY 10020

ISBN: 0-671-89428-5

First Archway Paperback printing February 1996

10 9 8 7 6 5 4 3 2 1

FEAR STREET is a registered trademark of Parachute Press, Inc.

AN ARCHWAY PAPERBACK and colophon are registered trademarks of Simon & Schuster Inc.

Cover art by Bill Schmidt

Printed in the U.S.A.

IL 7+

TheFace

prologue

I had a dream that I was drawing a silver line.

My sketch pad was propped against a white wall. And as I stared at the white paper, my hand moved slowly, steadily. And the line that I drew stretched across the page in silver.

Gleaming silver.

Cold silver.

I drew another silver line. And then a circle.

I pulled the page from the pad and smoothed my hand over the clean sheet beneath it. Then I started to draw another silver line.

In the dream, I felt a chill as the silver line stretched over the page.

I suddenly felt so cold.

Silver is a cold color. Cold as metal. Gray as winter.

Such a strange dream, I remember thinking in my dream.

I knew I was dreaming. I knew I couldn't really be drawing in such glittering silver.

I started a new line. Straight and very slender. A fine, silver line.

And as the line cut across the page, color seeped from it.

The color red.

A deep red seeped out from both sides of the silver line. Wet and glistening, the red spread over the page.

The silver line cut into the paper.

And the paper bled. The dark color spread, spread until it covered the white page.

And I woke from the dream, woke up screaming.

Why did I scream?

It was just a silver line.

Just a drawing of silver and red.

Just a dream.

So why did I scream?

I don't remember.

I really don't remember.

chapter

1

After the accident, I guess I went into shock.

I lost a part of my memory. A piece of my past life just slipped away from me.

I don't remember anything about that week. Or the weeks that followed.

I see last fall and the early part of the winter as a dark blur. It's like watching a dim reflection in the murky waters of a deep pond.

I can see ripples. But I'm not sure of the faces. Or the movements of the dark, watery figures.

What happened that week? That day?

Why don't I remember the accident?

Dr. Sayles says my memory will return. One day

the events of that week will come back, sharp and clear.

Dr. Sayles tells me not to rush it. Sometimes I think he doesn't *want* me to remember.

Maybe it's all too horrible. Maybe I'll be sorry if I know the truth.

Maybe I'm better off not remembering. Should I be thankful for the big hole in my memory?

Dr. Sayles tells me to go on with my life. And I try to.

But my friends aren't quite the same.

Sometimes I see Justine staring at me, her pale blue eyes narrowed. As if she's studying me, trying to pry into my brain.

Adriana is always telling me to take it easy. "Take it easy, Martha." As if I'm sick. Some kind of invalid.

Justine and Adriana seem so careful around me. They're always exchanging glances that I'm not supposed to see. They always seem to be watching me so carefully.

Watching for *what?*

Watching for me to crack? Watching for poor Martha to crack open like an egg and all my insides come running out in a yellow goo?

I've had strange thoughts since the accident last fall.

I can't help it.

Dr. Sayles says it's perfectly normal.

That's me. Martha Powell. Perfectly normal. I guess I *look* normal enough. I'm average height and

I weigh about one-twenty. About right for a high school junior.

I'm kind of preppy looking. I'm more J. Crew than grunge.

I have blond hair, long and very straight. Olive eyes. Big and round. My best feature. And light freckles on my cheeks that make me look about twelve years old!

I guess I have a nice smile. I don't smile as much as I used to.

But despite my weird thoughts, despite the holes in my brain, I guess I look okay.

I'm not beautiful and dark and exotic looking like Adriana. And I'd love to have Justine's thick tangles of red hair, her full red lips, and her round, pale blue eyes.

But I look okay.

At least Aaron thinks so.

Good old Aaron. He's been so loyal to me. So caring.

I don't know what I would do without him. I'm so lucky that I've been going with him for so long.

Justine reminds me just how lucky I am nearly every day. She's a good friend. But she doesn't try to hide her jealousy.

"Aaron is so *great!*" Justine gushed a few afternoons ago. "Check out that bod!"

"Justine, give me a break," I groaned.

We were in the gym bleachers at Shadyside High, watching a wrestling match against Waynesbridge. Aaron isn't exactly an all-state wrestler. He's big and athletic looking. But he doesn't work out as much as he should.

The guy he was wrestling was short and heavy and hairy. He looked like a bear. He had Aaron down on the mat in some kind of arm hold.

Aaron's face was bright red. He didn't look too happy.

Justine gripped tangles of red hair in both hands. She had an intense expression, as if she were wrestling along with Aaron.

Somehow Aaron spun out of his opponent's armlock. He pulled the hairy guy down. They were both grunting, both red-faced now. Aaron pinned him and jumped to his feet.

"Wow!" Justine cried, clapping hard. "Wow! Way to go, Aaron!"

Aaron was breathing hard. Even from the bleachers, I could see the sweat pouring down his forehead, matting his brown hair.

He helped pull his opponent up from the mat. Then he raised his head and flashed me a smile.

I mean, I *think* he was smiling at me.

Justine smiled and waved back, as if he were smiling at her!

At least Justine is honest about it. She doesn't try to hide how much she likes Aaron.

She's always flirting with him, even though he's my boyfriend. He flirts back sometimes. You know. Kids around with her.

But I don't think he takes her seriously.

As I said, he's been so loyal to me. So wonderful.

All of my friends have been wonderful.

If only they wouldn't walk on tiptoes around me. If only they wouldn't be so careful of what they say.

I know what they're thinking about. I know what's on their minds.

They probably wonder if my memory has snapped back.

But they're afraid to ask.

They won't talk about that week last November. About the accident. They never talk about it in front of me.

Maybe they don't want to remember it, either.

Maybe they think I'm the lucky one. Maybe they wish they could lose their memories too.

But I don't think I'm so lucky. Because the questions are driving me crazy.

What happened that night?

How horrible was it?

And why was *I* the one who went into shock?

chapter

2

I pressed my cheek against Aaron's shoulder. I liked the smell of his aftershave. Cool and sweet.

The first time he used it, I laughed at him. He only shaves about twice a week. But he splashes on the aftershave every day.

After a while I started to like it.

I raised my head and kissed him.

We had to be fast. We were sitting on the green leather couch in Aaron's den, and his little brother Jake was lurking about. If Jake saw us kissing, he'd probably wake up the whole house. That's the kind of kid he is. Your basic brat.

The TV was on. One of the *Lethal Weapon* movies. I like Mel Gibson. I think Aaron looks a little like him. Aaron has the same wavy brown hair and the same twinkling blue eyes.

But we weren't paying any attention to the movie. Aaron had his arm around my shoulders, and we were trying to sneak in a few kisses before Jake came bursting in.

Watching a dark-haired actress on the screen, I found myself suddenly thinking about Adriana.

"I'm kind of worried about Adriana," I confided.

Aaron grunted.

We kissed.

I heard footsteps behind us.

"Jake—is that you?" Aaron called, glancing back over his shoulder to the den doorway.

I heard giggling out in the hall. Jake is a major giggler.

"Get lost," Aaron ordered him.

"Make me." Jake's favorite reply.

"Okay. I will!" Aaron jumped up from the couch and started to the door. I heard another giggle. Then Jake's heavy footsteps as he ran away.

"Aaron was kissing Martha! Aaron was kissing Martha!" Jake chanted.

Shaking his head, Aaron dropped back beside me on the couch. On the TV screen a powerful explosion sent a building toppling to the ground.

Aaron grabbed a handful of nacho chips from the bowl beside him. He offered me the bowl. I waved it away.

"Adriana has gotten so skinny," I continued. "I'm really worried about her."

9

"Yeah. I know," Aaron replied with a mouthful of chips.

I sighed. "You know, I think the accident affected Adriana more than anyone."

Aaron swallowed. He kept his eyes on the TV screen. He didn't like it when I brought up the accident.

"She's lost so much weight," I repeated. "And did you see the dark circles around her eyes?"

"She's always had those," Aaron insisted, reaching for more chips.

"No way," I told him. "She had to go to a doctor because she can't sleep at night."

"Probably out partying," Aaron joked.

I gave his shoulder a hard shove. "Shut up."

He shrugged and kept his eyes on Mel Gibson.

That's what Aaron always does when I try to bring up anything serious, anything about the accident. He makes a joke.

He refuses to discuss it. I can see his whole body tense up. It makes him so uncomfortable.

Which drives me crazy. I'm *dying* to discuss it. I *need* to discuss it.

Also, I'm really worried about Adriana.

"Her grades are really suffering," I continued. "She didn't even make honor roll this term."

Aaron grunted in reply.

"You know that Adriana likes to be perfect," I reminded him. "You know how competitive she is. I know it must really upset her. She got a C in

Spanish! Do you believe it? That's her easiest course!"

Aaron shook his head. "She's messed up," he murmured.

He slid his arm around my shoulders. I snuggled against him, thinking about Adriana. When I kissed him, his lips tasted like nacho chips.

The movie ended on the TV. The credits rolled across the screen.

"Did you talk to her?" Aaron asked.

"Huh?" I didn't know what he meant.

"Did you talk to Adriana? About losing weight and everything?"

I sighed. "You know Adriana," I said, squeezing Aaron's hand. "I tried. But she refuses to talk to me about it. She won't discuss any of her problems with me."

Aaron frowned. "I thought you two were such close friends."

"We are," I insisted. "But Adriana never wants to talk about herself. Instead, she's always worrying about me. Always trying to cheer me up. Always trying to help me. Whenever I try to bring up anything serious with her, she just tells me everything will be fine."

Aaron nodded. He reached for the chips, then changed his mind. A serious expression settled over his handsome face. He locked his blue eyes on mine. "Everything *will* be fine," he said softly.

I nodded.

That's what all my friends kept telling me.

We kissed again. His lips still tasted salty. I didn't want him to pull away. I wanted the kiss to last forever.

But we heard giggling behind us. "I'm telling!" Jake declared.

Aaron jumped up to chase him away again.

I could hear them running down the hall, giggling and shouting.

I settled back on the couch, shut my eyes, and thought about Adriana.

Justine and Aaron had pretty much returned to normal. Why was Adriana so much more troubled than they?

Why had that night affected Adriana more than any of us?

Of course, I couldn't answer the question. I still had no memory of anything that had happened.

But I was determined to learn the answers.

So much to learn. So much.

So many surprises in store.

And then, the next afternoon, Adriana's brother tried to kill me.

chapter
3

*I*van Petrakis, Adriana's older brother, looks so much like his sister, it's scary.

They both have black hair, sort of wavy, sort of curly. Both of them are tall and thin and graceful. Both have soft brown eyes under heavy, black eyebrows. Their faces are dramatic. They stand out in our class photos.

Ivan adopted a new look this year. He had one ear pierced and wears a silver stud in it. And he let his sideburns grow long and grew a black goatee under his chin, which drives his parents crazy.

He wears black T-shirts and black denims, which make him look kind of tough. Not like the other kids from North Hills, the wealthiest neighborhood in Shadyside.

Lately, Ivan has been getting into trouble. At least, that's the rumor I heard from some guys who used to hang out with him. They say that he's messed up. That he's been drinking at parties and hanging out with some bad-news kids from Waynesbridge.

But I've always liked Ivan. Actually, I had a secret crush on him in third grade, and I don't know if I ever got over it.

When I ran into him at the Division Street Mall after school, I was glad to see him. "Hey—Ivan!" I called, rushing across the parking lot aisle. "What's up?"

He did an exaggerated reaction of surprise, throwing out his hands and nearly falling over backward. "Martha. Whoa. What did you buy? Anything to eat? Any Snickers bars? Milky Ways? I forgot to eat lunch."

I raised the two shopping bags I was carrying and motioned to the store behind me. "Just art supplies."

He groaned. "You still doodling?"

"Hey—!" I uttered a sharp cry. "I'm serious about my drawing, Ivan. It's not doodling."

That struck him funny. He let out his usual laugh. Sort of a hooting sound that made his slender shoulders go up and down.

"What are you doodling these days, Martha?"

"Shut up," I replied.

He hooted again. Scratched the tuft of fuzzy black hair under his chin. "Want a ride home?"

"Yeah. Sure." I followed him to his red Civic. He sort of strutted as he walked. Like some kind of tall, stuck-up bird.

One headlight on the car was cracked, the fender dented around it. "What happened, Ivan? An accident?"

He shrugged. "I don't know." He pulled open the driver's door and lowered his long body into the tiny car.

I tossed my two bags into the backseat, then climbed in beside him. The car smelled of cigarette smoke. I saw candy wrappers all over the floor.

This will give me a chance to talk about Adriana, I decided as Ivan backed out of the parking space. Maybe Ivan will have some ideas about how to help her.

He guided the car to the exit, then pulled out onto Division Street. "Want to run away?" he asked suddenly.

"Excuse me?" I turned to stare at him.

"Want to drive off and just keep driving?" he asked, returning my stare with those intense brown eyes. "Never turn back? Just keep driving in a straight line till we can't drive anymore?"

I let out a short, uncertain laugh. "You're joking—right?"

His expression didn't change.

"You don't really want to run away—do you?" I demanded, feeling my chest tighten.

He turned back to the windshield. "Whatever," he murmured.

He had to slam on the brakes to keep from plowing through a red light. We squealed to a stop in the middle of the crosswalk. The car behind us honked.

"Just joking," Ivan muttered. He tapped the wheel with both hands.

"How is Adriana?" I asked, eager to change the subject. Ivan seemed really tense, really wound up. "Has she been sleeping any better?"

The light changed. He lowered his foot on the gas pedal, and the car shot forward with a squeal. "I don't know. Ask her."

He sounded so bitter.

"I'm worried about her," I confessed. "She told me she hasn't been sleeping. Or eating."

"Boo-hoo." He scowled.

I shot him an angry look. But his eyes were on the road. It was about five-thirty—rush hour—and the streets were jammed with cars.

"You're her brother. Don't you worry about her?" My question burst out more shrill than I had planned.

He shrugged again. He seemed to talk mainly with his shoulders. "She's okay," he replied in a low, flat tone. "She went to a doctor last week. She taught her self-hypnosis or something."

"Excuse me?" A truck roared past. I wasn't sure I'd heard correctly.

"You know," Ivan said, shouting over the truck noise. "She hypnotizes herself. To help her sleep."

"Wow," I replied. Dumb. I know. But I wasn't sure what to say. "Is it safe?" I asked finally.

Ivan didn't seem to hear me. He made a left onto Park Drive.

The sky darkened nearly to black. Only five-thirty, and it already looked like the middle of the night. I hate February.

"Adriana's grades—" I started.

But Ivan interrupted with a hoarse cry. "It isn't easy to sleep at my house, Martha!" he shouted, slapping the steering wheel. "Nothing is easy at my house these days."

I knew that Ivan's parents weren't getting along. The rumor was that Mr. Petrakis had threatened to move out.

"Your parents—?" I asked meekly. I didn't really want to get into it. I mean, it really wasn't my business.

"It's a war zone," Ivan declared, shaking his head. Even in the dim light I could see his dull eyes, see the bitter scowl on his face. Bitter, yet mixed with fear.

"Last night they started throwing things at each other," he said, keeping his eyes straight ahead on the road.

"Oh, no," I murmured.

"Like babies. They started heaving plates and glasses at each other. Broken china all over the kitchen. I—I tried to stop them. It was so stupid. I—" Ivan's voice broke.

17

I let out a long sigh. "How awful," I murmured. "Then what happened?"

"Mom went running into the bedroom, crying and shrieking her head off. Dad stormed out. Slammed the door. I don't think he came back last night. At least, I didn't hear him."

"Is your mom okay?" I asked, squeezing the door handle.

Ivan swallowed hard. "I don't know. I heard her sobbing all night. Their bedroom is right next to mine." He lowered his voice to keep it from cracking again. "Bad break for me, huh?"

I didn't know what to say. Ivan's parents had been battling for months. Adriana gave me reports almost daily. They fought and fought, but neither would move out.

No wonder Adriana and Ivan were so nervous and crazy.

I peered out the window at the dark trees and houses whirring past us. Whirring past so rapidly.

A blur of black shadows against blackness.

I realized Ivan was driving too fast.

"Ivan, please—" I started.

We bolted through the stop sign at Canyon Drive. He didn't seem to notice.

"Ivan—slow down!" I cried.

"I—I just can't take it anymore!" Ivan shrieked. His eyes were wild. He gripped the top of the wheel with both hands. "It's too much, Martha! Too much!"

"Ivan—no!"

I gasped in horror as he let out another cry.

And spun the wheel hard.

"I can't take it!" His words a wail of pain, shouted over the roar of the engine.

The car squealed, tires scraped as he floored the gas pedal.

Spun the wheel. Spun the car.

Spun us.

Spun us around.

And aimed.

Screaming the whole time. Screaming out the pain from deep inside him.

Screaming as we spun.

I covered my eyes as the enormous black trunk of a tree loomed in the headlights. Ivan was heading us toward it.

Ivan is trying to kill us.

My last thought. My last thought on earth.

chapter

4

"**O**h!" My head hit the roof hard as we bounced over the curb. A shock of pain shuddered down my body.

We bounced again. And again.

And slowed to a stop.

I uncovered my eyes.

My hands shook. My whole body trembled.

I gasped for breath, trying to slow my pounding heart. I rubbed my head, still throbbing in pain.

"Ivan—"

"I'm sorry, Martha!" he cried.

"We're alive," I murmured. The words tumbled out. I wasn't thinking clearly. It was all still a blur. A dark, bouncing blur.

"We're alive, Ivan."

"I'm so sorry." A sob escaped his throat.

And without realizing it, I had turned. And I was holding him. Holding him in my arms. Feeling his body shake beneath his leather coat.

"We're alive."

"I turned the wheel. I—I couldn't do it. I couldn't go through with it," he stammered.

I held him tightly, pressing my cheek against his. "We're alive. We're alive." I couldn't stop chanting it.

"I wasn't really going to do it," Ivan murmured, his voice shaking. "Not really. I wouldn't do it."

I could feel him start to calm down. If only *my* heart would slip down from my throat!

"I'm okay," he said abruptly, almost coldly.

He pushed me away. "I'm okay now, Martha. Really."

I slumped back into my seat and glanced out the window. We were in the middle of someone's front yard. A porchlight cast yellow light over the front door. But the house was dark.

"Ivan, maybe you shouldn't drive," I managed to choke out.

"I'm okay now. Really. I'm fine. I'm fine."

A hard, cold look tightened his handsome face. He narrowed his eyes. Stone-faced now. As if he were fighting away all feelings.

He slammed the car into Reverse, and we bounced back onto the street.

His face remained frozen in that cold stare as he drove me home.

He didn't say another word.

"Your brother is really messed up," I told Adriana.

It was Saturday afternoon, and we were up in my room. A gray February afternoon. Dark clouds threatening snow.

I had the window open despite the cold. My room is always hot. The cool air felt good. A strong breeze fluttered the curtains.

"Huh?" Adriana sat at my dressing table, trying out blusher and lip gloss and other stuff from a new makeup kit my mom had given me. "This is too pale for me, don't you think?"

I cleared off my desk and set down a large drawing pad. I planned to sketch this afternoon. Some self-portraits maybe. Adriana's visit was a surprise.

She seemed bored. Kind of restless.

I kept saying things, but she only half-heard me. I wondered what was really on her mind. But I didn't really feel like asking her.

"Ivan is not in good shape," I repeated. "Yesterday afternoon—"

"Who *is* in good shape?" Adriana interrupted bitterly. She pulled out a handful of tissues and started wiping the blusher off her cheek. "I have such dark skin. This just doesn't work."

I turned and studied her reflection in the mirror. "You look kind of tired," I said.

22

"I still can't sleep." She shook her head. Started to apply a shiny lip gloss onto her full lips. A gust of wind fluttered her dark, curly hair.

"Ivan said you went to a doctor," I said, trying to sound casual. Adriana didn't like for people to pry. Even a good friend like me.

I think she was embarrassed about her family problems. Her parents' endless battles were humiliating to her. She gave me almost daily reports. But I never got the feeling she wanted me to question her about it. So I didn't.

She sighed, staring at herself in the mirror. "Her name is Dr. Corben. She's trying to teach me self-hypnosis. You know. To help me get to sleep. Sometimes I can do it. Sometimes it doesn't work."

She yawned as she started to rub off the lip gloss. "I have to keep practicing."

I watched her reach for another tube. Then I flipped through the blank pages of the drawing pad. I opened the desk drawer and pulled out a handful of charcoal pencils.

"Do you have the history notes?" Adriana asked, turning to face me.

'Excuse me?" I couldn't hide my surprise. "You want *my* notes?" Adriana was the straight-A student. Not me. She'd never asked for any notes of mine before.

Pink circles formed on her cheeks. She turned away. "I—I haven't been able to concentrate too well in class. You know. I've been so tired and everything. I missed some things."

23

She seemed so embarrassed. So . . . troubled.

I pulled my history notebook from my backpack and handed it to her. "Here. No problem."

"Hey, thanks." She stood up to leave. I took a step back. She's so much taller than I am. I always feel like a ten-year-old next to her.

I followed her to the door, still troubled about Ivan. Still hoping to tell her how messed up he was.

"Ivan gave me a ride home yesterday," I said. "Adriana, I think he needs some kind of help. He seemed really out of control. I mean—"

She turned at the bedroom door. "Martha, come on. You know what my brother's problem is." She rolled her eyes.

"Huh?" I searched her face, trying to figure out what she meant.

"Ivan's problem is Laura," Adriana explained.

"You mean—"

"Ever since Laura broke up with him, Ivan has been acting like a total jerk. Sometimes I just want to smash him!" She swung the history notebook as if batting someone.

I thought about what Adriana was saying.

Laura Winter is another friend of ours. With her sleek, black hair and shimmery blue-gray eyes and perfect cheekbones, she is the most beautiful girl at Shadyside High.

Laura is so beautiful, she's had some national modeling jobs. Everyone at school is convinced that someday Laura will move to New York and become an actress or a modeling superstar.

Ivan never could believe that Laura wanted to go out with him. And neither could we.

When they started going together, it was the talk of the whole school.

I always thought that Ivan was more serious about their relationship than Laura. Going out with Laura helped him forget about the ugly battles at home.

I was never sure why Laura decided to go with Ivan. Every guy at Shadyside High had the hots for her.

Then, sure enough, she dumped him last winter. She was pretty cold about it too. At least, that's what Adriana reported.

Ivan never talked about it with me.

"Ivan is still in shock," Adriana said, pressing the history notebook against the front of her sweater. "Months later, and he still can't believe that Laura isn't crazy about him."

"Has he called her?" I asked.

Adriana shook her head. "No way. He's so stuck up, I think he's waiting for *her* to call *him!*"

Adriana laughed. Sort of an empty laugh.

I didn't join in. Ivan had nearly killed us both the day before. I knew that his problems were no laughing matter.

"Adriana, someone should talk to Ivan," I said.

Her brown eyes flared. *"You* try to talk to him." Her voice sounded angry. "He's impossible. *No one* can talk to him."

"But, Adriana—" I protested.

Her expression softened. "Don't worry about him, Martha. Ivan can take care of himself. You're such a nice person. You worry about everyone but yourself."

She gripped the notebook with both hands. Her eyes locked on mine. "We all just want for you to be okay. Don't worry about Ivan."

She turned and disappeared down the stairs.

I started after her. "I *am* worried about Ivan. I don't think he can take care of himself. You don't realize how upset he is."

That's what I *wanted* to say to Adriana.

But I stopped in the hallway with a sigh. Adriana didn't want to discuss Ivan. She didn't want me interfering in her family life.

I stepped back into my room. The clouds outside the window had darkened to a deep charcoal color. The wind gusted, making the curtains flap against the wall.

It's freezing in here, I realized. I shut the window and straightened the curtains, pushing them back into place. Then I made my way across the room to my desk and sat down in front of my fresh, clean drawing pad.

I pulled back the cover and tucked it behind the pad. Then I sifted through the pile of charcoal pencils till I found the narrow point I wanted.

I always find a brand-new drawing pad kind of exciting. I mean, there it is. Empty and clean. Waiting to be filled up with something that's never been seen before.

I'm pretty talented as an artist. I have a good eye for drawing. And my line is pretty clean.

I take special art classes at the state college in Waynesbridge. My teachers all think my talent can be developed.

I'm trying to put a portfolio together. Mostly portraits. I need it to apply to the special summer art program at the college.

I rolled my desk chair away and slid it against the wall. I like to draw standing up.

I shut my eyes and tried to clear my mind. Tried to clear all thoughts about Ivan and Adriana from my mind. Tried to clear *all thoughts* from my mind.

Then I gazed down toward the desktop at the drawing pad, at the fresh, white sheet. Raised the pencil. And started to draw.

A face, I decided. I'll draw my face.

The pencil scratched against the surface of the paper. I started with eyes. I always start with eyes.

Whoa. Not my eyes.

The eyes I drew were oval. My eyes are kind of round.

Leaning over the desk, I gazed down at the eyes. They seemed to stare up at me.

I filled in the pupils. Dark pupils. Serious eyes.

I swept the pencil over the pad, creating a light outline of the head. The basic shape.

Not my head, I saw.

A slender face. With those dark, serious eyes.

"Hey—what's happening?" I murmured out loud. "Who are you?"

My hand moved quickly now, filling in details.

Wait. No.

What was happening?

The charcoal tip scratched the paper. It seemed to be moving on its own.

Out of my control.

My hand—it curled over the paper, moved in short circles, dipped and rose up. As if drawing by itself.

As if drawing without me.

As if guided by a ghostly hand, I continued to draw. Staring down in amazement—in fear—I let my hand finish the drawing.

I knew I couldn't stop it.

chapter

5

I was breathing hard by the time I finished the portrait. My hands were sweaty, my fingers cramped.

I don't know how long it took. But I knew that I'd never drawn anything that fast in all my life.

Resting both hands on the desktop, I leaned over the pad and stared down at the face I had drawn.

A boy's face.

Not someone I knew.

Not someone I recognized.

He had wavy, dark hair. One tangle of it fell over his narrow forehead.

He had those dark, serious eyes. Gloomy eyes. Deep, troubled eyes.

The nose didn't go with the eyes. It was too small and kind of turned up.

I lowered my gaze and discovered that I had drawn him smiling. The smile didn't go at all with the gloomy eyes. He had a pleasant smile. Thin lips. A small cleft in his chin.

"Wow," I murmured.

Was this someone I had seen before?

He didn't look at all familiar.

Was it just a made-up face? Not the face of a real person? Just a creation of my imagination?

I studied it closely, still breathing hard. Still feeling the pull of the invisible force that guided my hand.

The portrait had so many details. The face seemed like such a real face. Such a *specific* face.

I studied the dark strand of hair falling so casually over the forehead. My eyes scanned lower. I had drawn a dark, round mole on the boy's right cheek.

A mole?

I had never drawn a mole before on any of the portraits I had done, imaginary or real.

Never.

"What *is* this?" I asked myself.

And then my eyes stopped on the left eyebrow.

A tiny, white scar divided the eyebrow in two.

That detail made me gasp. It was so real. So distinct. Could I have created that scar from my imagination?

Maybe. But why hadn't I ever drawn a scar like that before?

I leaned over the portrait. "Who are you?" I asked it.

The dark eyes stared up at me. The boy's thin-lipped smile revealed nothing. Nothing at all.

With a low cry, I tore the page from the pad. Then I crumpled it into a ball and tossed it in the trash can beside the desk.

My hands still felt cold and clammy. The back of my neck tingled.

My throat had tightened. In fear?

I didn't want that drawing around. I didn't want to see that unfamiliar face.

I wanted to draw my own portrait.

I wiped my hands on the legs of my jeans. Then I sifted through the charcoal pencils, searching for one with a broader point.

I carried the small, square mirror on my dressing table to the desk and stood it up beside my drawing pad. Inspecting myself in the mirror, I straightened my blond bangs. And wiped a smudge of charcoal off my cheek.

I'm not going to draw my freckles, I decided. I'm going to pretend they aren't there. I'm going to pretend that I have smooth, creamy skin like Laura.

Laura.

I felt tempted to call Laura. I wanted to draw her for the portfolio. I had drawn her before. Those high, perfect cheekbones were so much fun to draw.

Laura is so vain, I told myself. My drawings never satisfied her. She claimed I made her look like a brainless bimbo. "Martha, why do I always look like such an airhead in your drawings?" she demanded after our last session.

"I paint what I see," I teased.

She didn't smile. She always takes herself so seriously.

I guess if I looked as beautiful as Laura, I'd take myself seriously too.

She made me change her smile, over and over. I never could get it right.

Now I turned back to my own face in the mirror. "I'm going to make you as sophisticated as Laura," I told myself.

I leaned over the pad and started to draw.

Began with the eyes.

No. Wait.

Not those eyes.

My hand moved rapidly, out of my control.

Out of control.

The slender outline of the face.

The dark eyes. The wavy hair. The turned-up nose.

"Wait. No!"

I was drawing the boy again. The same face.

I felt a chill. A cold tingle of fear that swept down the back of my neck.

"No way!"

I tore the page out of the pad without finishing the portrait. I didn't bother to crumple it up. I sailed it across the desk and watched it float to the floor.

I took a deep breath. And ignoring the trembling of my hand, started to draw again.

This time I kept my eyes on the mirror. Watched my reflection as I drew. Determined to draw myself.

My own face. Not that boy's face. *My* face.

But it was no use. My hand wouldn't cooperate.

"No! Please no!" I uttered an alarmed cry as my arm moved on its own. My hand dipped and glided. Sketching. Scratching. Filling in the details.

The details of the boy's face.

The cleft in the chin. The mole. The round, black mole. And now the scar. The slender, white scar cutting through one eyebrow. The black eyebrows, arched just slightly over the dark, brooding eyes.

"No way!" I ripped out the drawing and flung it to the floor beside the other one.

I quickly brought the cover of the drawing pad down. I shoved the pencils into the drawer.

My heart pounded. I wiped my clammy hands on my jeans legs again.

And stared down at the two drawings on the floor. The two faces. Of the same boy. The same unknown boy.

"Who *are* you? Who?"

He stared up at me. As if trying to answer. As if trying to tell me something.

Trying to tell me *what?*

"Why am I drawing you? Why can't I draw what I want?"

I bent down. Grabbed up both sheets of paper. And ripped them.

Ripped them again and again. Ripped them into narrow shreds.

And asked myself: *Am I cracking up? Am I totally cracking up?*

chapter

6

That night I hurried to meet Aaron at the mall at eight o'clock. We had a date for the eight-thirty movie. He works a weekend shift behind the counter at Pete's Pizza. Aaron's father is friends with the owner or something. Aaron usually gets off work a little before eight.

I had trouble finding a parking space near the movie theater. I finally had to park all the way at the other end, near the Doughnut Hole.

I started jogging across the lot when I realized I'd left my headlights on. "Aaaagh!" I let out a frustrated groan and went running back.

By the time I finally made it to the theater, it was a few minutes after eight. The lobby was packed with people. I think I saw half of Shadyside High as I searched for Aaron.

I spotted him finally at the side of the popcorn counter. And to my surprise, I saw Justine too.

She had an arm draped casually around Aaron's shoulders. And they were laughing about something with their heads pretty close together.

What is *this* about? I asked myself.

Justine always flirts with Aaron when I'm around. They're always teasing each other and kidding around.

But I never stopped to think that she flirts with him when I'm *not* around.

Watching them laugh together, with her arm around his shoulders as if she owned him, gave me sort of a sick feeling.

Justine was my friend, after all. I didn't want to start having evil thoughts about her.

I made my way through the crowd and hurried over to them. Justine dropped her arm from Aaron's shoulders and took a step back when she saw me.

"Hey. How's it going?" Aaron asked. He flashed me his great smile. It instantly made me feel better.

"Okay," I said. I had decided in the car not to tell him about my strange afternoon, about the face I kept drawing almost against my will.

Aaron has been through so much unhappiness with me since the accident. He's been so good to me, so understanding about my memory loss.

Sometimes I don't tell him upsetting things that are on my mind. I don't want him to think that I'm crazy or anything.

"What's up?" I asked him cheerfully. I took his hand. I really was glad to see him.

"The usual. I had to work." He motioned to several dark tomato sauce stains on his sweatshirt. "Can't you tell?"

I laughed. "You smell like a pizza too. Yum."

"I was shopping and ran into Aaron," Justine chimed in. She twirled a ringlet of red hair around one finger. "He said you wouldn't mind if I tagged along to the movies."

"Of course not," I replied quickly. *Just keep your paws off him!* I thought.

Then I felt bad for thinking it.

"I have the tickets. Let's go in," Aaron said.

"We need popcorn," Justine insisted. She made her way into the line at the counter.

A few minutes later she returned with an enormous bucket of buttery popcorn. "I got a small!" she joked.

Aaron guided me by the shoulders into the theater. The trailers had already started. We found seats near the front. I always like to sit as close as possible. I don't like people in front of me. I like to lose myself in the screen.

Aaron sat between me and Justine with the bucket of popcorn on his lap. Justine and I helped ourselves.

A couple of times I saw Justine's hand brush against Aaron's. I wondered if it was deliberate.

Each time she touched him, I felt a cold chill.

My phone rang a little after midnight. Startled, I grabbed up the receiver before the end of the first ring. "Hello?"

"Hi, it's me."

"Justine?" I couldn't hide my surprise. Aaron and I had just dropped her home half an hour earlier. "Are you okay?"

"Yeah. Fine. I . . . just wanted to talk."

I yawned and glanced at the clock. *What is Justine's problem?* I asked myself. *I spent the whole night with her.*

"We didn't really get a chance to talk," she explained. "Pretty dumb movie, huh?"

I carried the phone across the room and dropped down onto the edge of my bed. "Jim Carrey was funny," I replied. "He's so gross. He always makes me laugh."

"Aaron laughed so hard, I thought he was going to choke!" Justine exclaimed.

"You know Aaron," I said, straightening the sleeve of the long T-shirt I usually sleep in.

And then I thought: *How well do you know Aaron, Justine?*

"He's usually the only one laughing at these movies," I continued, shaking my bitter thought from my mind. "Aaron laughs at anything. Especially if it's gross."

There was a long silence at Justine's end. Then she blurted out, "I'm really so jealous of you."

"Excuse me?"

My cat, Rooney, jumped up beside me on the bed. I gently pushed her back to the floor. She leaves white fur over everything.

"You heard me," Justine said sharply. "I said I'm jealous. Aaron is such a great guy."

"Yeah. He is," I replied. Pretty lame. I admit it. But I didn't know what else to say.

I mean, what could I say to Justine? *Is that why you're coming on to him all the time?* I could never say that. She's my friend.

And tonight she sounded kind of troubled.

"Are you okay?" I asked.

Another silence. I could hear her pacing back and forth in her room. I pictured her in pajamas, her red hair loose over her shoulders.

"Guess I'm a little down," she admitted, speaking softly.

"What's wrong?" I demanded, pushing Rooney off the bed again. I leaned down to pet the cat, but she scurried out of my room.

"Nothing really. Everything. Nothing. Everything," Justine replied. She loved talking in puzzles.

I waited for her to explain.

"I just started thinking about things tonight. Before the movie," she continued. "You know. Different things. I had this long talk with my parents."

Uh-oh, I thought. Justine's parents were the gloomiest, most depressing people in the world.

"You know I can't go to college next fall." Justine sighed. "There's just no money. And my grades aren't good enough for a scholarship."

She let out a bitter laugh. "I couldn't get a scholarship to Waynesbridge Junior College!"

The junior college is kind of a joke with Shadyside kids. We all call it High School II!

"So I have to stay home and work for a couple of years," Justine continued. "You know. Save my money." She sighed again.

"It's a bad break," I agreed. "But it isn't the end of the world, Justine. I mean—"

"You're lucky, Martha," she interrupted. "You have nice parents. And they have enough money. You have Aaron. You've got really good grades. You're a talented artist—"

"Justine—stop!" I cried, jumping to my feet. "You're wrong. I know you *think* I have a *perfect* life. But—"

"No, I don't," Justine cut in.

"Huh?" Her reply surprised me.

"No, I don't, Martha," she repeated. And then her voice became strange. Kind of tight. And cold. "Your life isn't as perfect as you think," she said.

I took a deep breath. "What do you mean?" I demanded, almost shyly.

Silence.

"Justine—what did you mean by that?"

"I've got to go," she whispered. "My dad is shouting at me to get off the phone."

"But wait—" I insisted.

I heard a click, and the line went dead.

I tossed the phone onto the bed. Crossed my arms in front of me. Tapped my bare foot on the rug.

"Your life isn't as perfect as you think."

What did she mean by that remark?

Something about Aaron? Something about Aaron and Justine?

Or was it something much worse?

chapter

7

"Come on, Rooney. Come here." I patted my lap.

I was stretched out on the couch in the den in torn jeans and an old sweatshirt, and I felt like holding Rooney and petting her. But of course she wouldn't come near me.

Why do cats always have to act like cats?

It was Sunday evening, and I was feeling pretty lonely. Mom and Dad were visiting friends across town. I finished my homework early. There was no school the next day, anyway. Some kind of teachers' meetings.

I called Laura to see if she wanted to hang out or something. Not home. Adriana wasn't home either.

So now I was stretched out in the den, half-watching wet snow drizzle down outside the window, half-watching a skiing show on ESPN on the TV across the room.

"Rooney—come here!"

The cat turned and strutted away with her tail in the air.

I settled back against the couch arm. And gazed up at the TV screen.

And saw a cabin. A wooden cabin surrounded by snow. Snow tumbling off the sloping roof.

"Oh!"

I sat up.

My head was spinning. I felt dizzy.

A flash. A flash of memory.

The cabin. The snow. I was starting to remember.

I jumped to my feet. My heart was pounding. I suddenly felt cold all over. As if I were in that snow. As if I were standing outside that snow-covered wooden cabin.

I shut my eyes, struggling to concentrate. Struggling to pull more memory back.

I had a picture in my mind. The scene on the TV had brought back a picture. But I needed more than a picture. I needed to remember *more*.

Keeping the snowy cabin in my mind, trying not to lose the strange feeling, I hurried upstairs to my room. I dropped down at my desk. Shut my eyes again.

And tried to drift into the scene. Tried to slide

myself into the snow. Tried to see everything. To remember . . .

Whoa. Two cabins. I saw two cabins side by side.

Snow piled up against the cabin walls. Drifts sloping up to the curtained windows. The windows glowing golden, reflecting the bright sunlight.

The snow glowing too. Everything so bright and clear and cold.

Where am I? I wondered. Do I know these two cabins? Have I been there?

Is this real memory? A piece of memory coming back?

Or is it imagination?

I tried not to think. I just wanted to see.

And I did start to see. I saw some colorful figures, a bright blur in the shimmering, silvery snow.

So hard to see in the bright glare. As if the white light had formed a curtain, a curtain hiding their faces from me.

I concentrated harder.

I stared at the colors moving over the snow. The colors formed themselves into people.

I saw four girls.

"Hey—!" I cried out as I recognized the girl in front.

Me. I recognized me. Recognized my long blond hair poking down from my blue wool ski cap. Recognized my blue-and-white ski suit.

Concentrate. Concentrate.

I forced myself deeper into the scene. Deeper into the memory.

And my three friends moved through the curtain of light, moved through the snow, into clear view. Adriana, Justine, and Laura.

They were there with me.

I could see their smiles. Could see their red cheeks. Could see their breath streaming up in front of them as they walked, boots crunching in the deep snow.

And suddenly we were inside the cabin.

Warm and bright. An orange fire blazing in the stone fireplace. Mugs of hot apple cider.

Yes. The four of us were sitting around the table. I could see the red-and-white-checkered tablecloth. The white mugs. They stuck to the plastic tablecloth when we lifted them.

The fire leaping, making our faces so golden.

And then a knock on the door. The wooden chairs scraping against the wooden floor.

Shouts from outside. More pounding on the door.

Who is it?

All four of us jump up. Adriana gets to the door first.

I can see her so clearly now.

She's wearing a bright yellow sweater, pulled down over navy ski pants. She has a headband in her black hair. Her face is still red from the cold.

She pulls open the cabin door. A blast of cold air. Sparkly crystals of snow in the air.

I see it all so clearly.

But who is at the door?

Aaron?

Yes. I see Aaron. I recognize his black, down ski parka. The black cap pulled over his dark hair.

Aaron is there. And two other boys.

Yes. Two boys.

But I can't see them. I can't see their faces.

The other two boys—why can't I see them?

I blinked. And the scene vanished.

As if someone had clicked off the light.

The boys. My friends. The orange fire. The mugs of cider. The cabin. The snow. All vanished.

I blinked again, then shut my eyes. I wanted to go back, back to the cabin. Back into my memory.

But I saw only swirling blackness.

I opened my eyes and lowered them to the desktop. "Huh?" I uttered a low cry when I realized I'd been drawing on the pad the whole time.

Without even realizing it, I had been sketching.

I raised the pad and studied it.

And saw to my horror that I had drawn the face again.

chapter

8

T he next morning, a blustery gray Monday, I woke up in time for school. Then remembered I had the day off.

I tried to get back to sleep, but couldn't. When I dragged myself up at about nine, I discovered Rooney curled up and sleeping soundly at the foot of the bed.

"Have you been there all night?" I asked her.

She didn't stir.

I spent the morning doing some errands for my mother. When I returned home a little after noon, I found Laura waiting for me in the kitchen.

"Hey—hi!" I couldn't hide my surprise. "What's up?"

She narrowed her perfect, blue-gray eyes at me.

"Did you forget? You promised you'd come with me today."

I stared hard at her, trying to remember.

Was my memory playing more tricks on me?

Laura wore a black leather vest, open over a dark brown turtleneck. The sweater came down nearly to her knees, over her loose black jeans. Her black hair was pulled into a simple ponytail that fell halfway down her back.

"The photo shoot," she said impatiently. She pulled open the refrigerator door and lifted out a small bottle of club soda. "Remember, Martha? You promised to come with me?"

"Oh, yeah. Right." It was starting to come back to me. Laura and I had made this plan weeks ago.

"I've never worked with this photographer before. And he has a studio in a crummy part of town in the Old Village. And my parents were too busy to take me, of course," Laura rattled on. "So I'd really feel better if you came with me. Okay?"

"Yeah. No problem," I replied.

I always felt like a Wordless Wonder next to Laura. She spoke in *avalanches*. The words tumbled out—and kept tumbling out until I felt snowed under!

She took a short sip from the club soda bottle. "Yuck. I hate this stuff. But at least it's no calories."

"There's some Diet Coke in there," I offered.

She shook her head. Took another sip. Then she brushed back her hair. "They told me not to do anything with my hair, so I just pulled it back. I guess they want to style it when I get there."

She set down the bottle and gazed at me. "Did you do something different with *your* hair today?"

I laughed. "No. The wind blew it when I went out. I forgot to brush it."

We both laughed.

"How's it going?" Laura asked, her expression turning serious. But she didn't wait for me to answer. "We'd better get going. I like to be early when I haven't worked with someone before. I mean, I know we'll just stand around waiting, anyway."

She sighed. "It takes these guys *hours* to get the lights right. And then some fuse always blows. But I don't want to be the one who causes the delay. I mean, I don't want anyone to complain to the agency. They've gotten me some good jobs so far."

She finally took a breath.

"Want to take my car?" I asked.

She took a final sip of club soda. "Yeah. Sure. Thanks." She pulled her dark blue parka over her shoulders. "Thanks for coming with me, Martha. It's great we'll have a chance to talk."

She'll have a chance to talk, I thought. *I'll* have a chance to *listen!*

A cold drizzle started to come down as we drove to the Old Village. The wipers scraped back and forth over the windshield. Some of the streets had iced up. But my old Volvo didn't slip or slide.

Laura told me about some new outfits she'd

bought at Dalby's Department Store. "I probably bought too much. But Dad says they're tax deductible if I wear them for a shoot. Did I tell you I may be up for a TV commercial in New York? A cousin of mine. Artie? I don't think you've met him. He knows a talent guy at some big agency there. He thinks he can get me an audition for a commercial, if I can get my portfolio in better shape."

The word *portfolio* made me think of my drawing pad. Of the face I had been drawing again and again. I wondered if Laura would recognize the face.

Last winter Dr. Sayles told my friends not to try to help me get my memory back. "It has to come back naturally," he told them. "Do not try to give Martha hints. Her mind must return to what happened in its own time."

But still I wondered if Laura would recognize the boy in my drawings.

The shoot went well. I watched from the side of the studio as Laura posed.

The photographer was a funny little man, skinny as a pencil, with a mop of white hair on his head. Dressed all in faded denim. He kept talking to himself, never stopped talking the whole time we were there. With his constant chatter, mostly under his breath, he even managed to get Laura quiet!

The photos were for a T-shirt company. Laura had to wear six different styles of T-shirts. The photographer's assistant, a pleasant young woman not much older than us, acted as stylist. She changed Laura's hair for each shot.

Laura looked beautiful, of course. And she appeared so comfortable in front of the camera. As if she'd been doing it her whole life.

She kept glancing over at me the whole time. "Martha—sure you're not bored?"

I assured her I was having a great time. This is as close as *I'll* ever come to a modeling studio! I realized.

Afterward, I drove Laura home. The drizzle had stopped, but the roads remained icy. The sky was as gray as evening.

"I went to a party last night," Laura told me, brushing her hair out, staring at herself in the little mirror in the window visor.

"I called you," I replied. "I wondered where you were."

"It was at Gary Brandt's house. His parents were away." She rolled her eyes. "Of course it got out of control."

"What happened?" I asked.

She dropped the hairbrush into her bag and pushed up the visor. "Ivan was there."

I glanced at her. Nearly went through a stop sign. "Really?"

"Ivan is really messed up," Laura groaned. "I mean, you wouldn't believe it. He drank so much beer—"

"He was drinking again?" I shook my head. Poor Ivan. I felt so bad for him.

"He drank so much, he started dancing—and he passed out," Laura reported.

She frowned. "He just fell over. Onto all the chips and food on the coffee table. And then he just lay there. In the food. What a mess. Stuff spilled all over the rug."

She tsk-tsked. "Gary and Bobby Newkirk and some of the other guys had to pick him up and stretch him out on the couch. I mean, he was really totaled."

"Wow," I murmured. "Bad news."

Laura made a disgusted face. "I can't believe I went out with him. I mean, what did I like about him? He's such a total jerk."

"Adriana says he's messed up because of you," I blurted out. "Because you dumped him."

Laura's mouth dropped open. Her pale cheeks turned crimson. "Whatever," she murmured.

"Don't you care?" I demanded.

She shook her head. "No way." Then she added, "He'll get over it."

I decided to change the subject. "Justine called me late on Saturday night. We talked for a long time. She seems really depressed, really down."

Laura turned in her seat to face me. "What did you tell her?" she demanded.

"Not much," I replied, pulling the car up Laura's driveway. "What could I tell her?"

Laura pushed open the car door and climbed

out. But instead of saying goodbye and closing the door, she leaned back into the car.

I was startled to see a strange, tense expression on her face. "Hey, Martha," she said, lowering her voice almost to a whisper.

"What?"

"Watch out for Justine."

chapter
9

The next day I paid my weekly visit to Dr. Sayles.

Dr. Sayles is young looking, with long, wavy blond hair, pale blue eyes, and a dimple in each cheek. He wears Polo shirts and chinos. He has broad shoulders and powerful-looking arms. I guess he works out.

He doesn't look like a shrink at all. I think he looks more like a surfer dude on *Baywatch*. But he's very smart, and he has helped me a lot.

His office isn't what I expected, either. He has a poster of Jimi Hendrix on the wall behind his desk. And he doesn't have a couch. Instead, he has two comfortable leather armchairs that face each other—one for the patient and one for him.

I like Dr. Sayles. But I can't say that I look forward to my sessions with him.

They're painful. Not because of what I remember about last November. But because of what I *can't* remember.

Sometimes I feel embarrassed by how little progress I've made. I mean, when I tell Dr. Sayles that I still don't remember anything, I feel as if I'm letting him down.

So today I felt excited. Today I sat tensely in the small waiting room, eager to get into the office.

Today I finally had something to tell him.

"I—I think my memory is starting to come back," I said as soon as I sat down. I felt so excited, so nervous, I stammered. I spread my clammy hands over the warm leather chair arms and silently instructed myself to calm down.

"Really?" Dr. Sayles swept his hand back through his blond hair. Then he tapped his pencil against the long yellow pad in his lap.

"Yes. I . . . saw something. A picture in my mind," I continued.

He leaned forward. His pale blue eyes searched my face, as if trying to read my thoughts. "What did you see, Martha?"

I swallowed. My mouth suddenly felt dry. I squeezed the chair arms. "I saw two cabins," I told him. "In the snow. I mean, it was very snowy. Snow on the ground. Snow on the cabin roofs. The cabin—it was on top of a hill. A very steep hill."

He nodded.

I instantly felt disappointed.

I don't know what I expected him to do. Jump out of his chair? Run over and hug me? Shout, "Yes! Yes! That's wonderful!"

I don't know what. But I expected more than a nod.

"That's good, Martha," he said finally. He nodded again. Then he scribbled something on the pad.

"Is it a real memory?" I asked eagerly. "Were there two cabins on top of a snowy hill? Did they have something to do with . . . with what happened?"

He ignored my questions. "What else did you see?"

I sighed. Why wasn't he more excited? Why wasn't he being more helpful?

"What else was in the picture?" he demanded quietly, tapping his pencil on the chair arm now.

I told him the rest. About seeing Justine, Laura, and Adriana. About seeing Aaron and two other boys. About how I couldn't see the other boys' faces.

Again, he nodded.

"Am I starting to remember? Is it coming back to me?" I asked impatiently.

"I think so," he replied. I waited for him to smile or show some emotion—*any* emotion. But he didn't.

I guess he was just being professional. But I wanted him to be *human*. I wanted him to help me.

"This is encouraging, Martha," he said finally. He crossed his long legs. He wore Bass Weejun loafers with white socks. "What else did you see?"

"That's about it." I tried to remember if I had seen more. But the picture had vanished from my mind before anyone in the cabin said or did anything.

"Oh!" I cried out, suddenly remembering the drawings I had brought.

He sat up straight. "What's wrong, Martha?"

I pulled my backpack up from the floor and started to unzip it. "I almost forgot. I brought you these."

I tugged out the sheets from my drawing pad and unfolded them. "Drawings I made," I told him. "Of a face."

I held one of the drawings up to him. "I keep drawing the same face, the same boy, over and over," I said. "I don't know why. It's almost as if I'm drawing against my will."

I held up two of the drawings, one in each hand.

"Do you recognize the boy, Dr. Sayles?" I demanded eagerly. "Do you?"

To my surprise, he was staring at the drawings with bulging eyes. His mouth wide open.

No longer the blank-faced professional.

He was staring at my drawings in total shock.

chapter

―――――

10

I finished my homework early on Saturday. I was kind of bored. Aaron was away visiting cousins with his family.

I sat in my room, listening to music drift up from downstairs. Dad had the Metropolitan Opera on the radio. He always played it cranked up really loud. My bedroom door was closed, but I could still hear it as if I were in the living room with him.

Outside the window the sky spread out, blue and clear. A mound of snow rose up on the outer sill, pressing against the window. It had snowed for two days. The sun had finally come out.

I stared down at a drawing of the boy's face. Stared into his serious eyes. Stared at the scar that split his eyebrow.

Who was he?

Why did I keep drawing him?

Why wouldn't Dr. Sayles tell me? And why did Dr. Sayles lose his cool? Why did he have such a startled expression on his face when I held up the drawing?

Questions. Questions.

I had a lot of questions. Not many answers.

I was still staring at the boy's face when the bedroom door flew open, and Laura and Adriana burst in.

"What's up?" Adriana cried.

"You can't stay in. You've got to come with us," Laura insisted.

They both had blue down jackets pulled down over faded jeans. They both carried round, red plastic sleds. Their cheeks were nearly as red as the sleds.

"Huh? What's going on?" I asked. I dropped the drawing to the desktop.

"It's gorgeous out!" Laura exclaimed. "The most beautiful day of the winter!"

"It's perfect sledding," Adriana chimed in excitedly. "The snow sort of froze. There's an icy crust on top. You've got to come to Miller Hill with us, Martha!"

I gaped at both of them. They were acting like ten-year-olds!

"You mean—you want to go sledding?"

They both laughed at me. I know I sounded like a moron. But I was so surprised.

"Why can't we have fun?" Laura demanded. "You know. Like we used to. Before we got old. Before we were supposed to start acting *cool* all the time?"

"Come on, Martha." Adriana tugged me off the chair. "Get your coat. It's not even that cold out. Come on. We've got an extra sled."

"We'll have races," Laura suggested. She helped Adriana push me to the door. "We'll push all the eight-year-old kids off the hill and have it all to ourselves!"

"Hey—why not?" I said finally. We pushed each other down the stairs, singing along with Dad's opera, singing so loud he shouted for us to shut up. Which made us laugh, and sing even louder.

Why *shouldn't* I have some fun? I asked myself.

Why should I sit up in my room staring at that creepy drawing?

I realized I hadn't had any fun . . . any *real* fun . . . since the accident. Since I lost my memory.

I grabbed my snow parka and a pair of woolly gloves and followed my two friends out the front door. They were right. It was a beautiful afternoon. The air felt cold and crisp. The bright sunlight made the snow sparkle like gold.

We walked to Miller Hill, carrying our round sleds, rolling them like hoops, sending them crashing into each other.

Nearly to the top of the street, Adriana slipped and fell. Laura and I pounced on her and pushed her face into the snow.

She sputtered. Came up laughing. And started a wild wrestling match that got all three of us wet and snow-covered.

Laughing, breathing hard from our strenuous battle, we brushed each other off. We gathered up our disks, which had slid halfway down the street. And continued on our way.

Miller Hill is the favorite sledding place in Shadyside. It's steep and bumpy and stretches into a wide, empty field. The snow always seems deeper and slicker on Miller Hill. It's a steep climb up. But the ride down is long, fast, and totally thrilling.

Today the hill glowed like a silvery mountain. Laura, Adriana, and I stopped at the bottom and gazed up. Dozens of kids, kids of all ages, were sledding down. On every kind of sled! Garbage can lids and inflated snow doughnuts competed with old-fashioned wood-and-steel Flexible Flyers.

What a scene!

In their red, and blue, and purple jackets, their snow hats and ski caps, the kids looked like Christmas ornaments on a huge, white tree.

I know. I know. I'm starting to sound like a poet or something.

But it was just such a thrilling sight. Such an *innocent* scene. I guess it made me think of being younger. It made me think of happier times.

"How come the hill looks so much bigger than it used to?" Laura asked, ducking out of the way as two little boys came sliding down on plastic garbage bags.

"Don't wimp out," Adriana scolded her. "The hill is the same as it always was. Let's go."

Slipping and sliding, we leaned into the wind and made our way up to the top of the hill. Halfway up, the wind from the top blew the plastic sled from my hand, and I had to go chase it.

I finally made it to the top.

Where were Laura and Adriana?

I shielded my eyes from the bright sunlight with one gloved hand and searched for them.

They were already preparing to slide down. They had found an open spot on one side, just past a group of serious-faced boys. Now they were lowering themselves onto their sleds.

Laura was sitting on hers. Adriana had plopped down on her belly.

I darted over, planning to surprise Adriana and give her a hard shove.

But they were too fast for me.

They both took off with happy squeals. The sleds dropped fast.

Laura hit a hard bump. Her sled flew into the air. But she managed to hold on.

Adriana reached the bottom and just kept going. Her sled took her halfway across the field below.

I laughed. What a great ride!

My turn, I told myself.

I tried to remember the last time I had stood up here on Miller Hill, the last time I had sledded down.

I was probably ten or eleven, I guessed.

Well, why should the ten-year-olds have all the fun?

I gazed down to the bottom of the hill—and saw Adriana and Laura standing together, sleds at their sides. Adriana had pulled off her ski cap and was brushing snow from her black hair. They were both staring up at me. Waiting for me to join them.

"Here I come!" I shouted, cupping my gloved hands around my mouth. I don't think they could hear me.

A gust of wind gave me a hard shove from behind.

I lowered my sled to the snow, resting it on the edge. Then I lowered myself to my knees.

I gripped the sides of the disk and dropped on top of it.

Another wind gust sent me sliding down. Before I was ready to go.

I nearly fell off as the disk slid down. Picked up speed. I bounced over a sharp bump. Held on.

Screaming.

Oh, no.

The white snow whirring past. A blizzard of white.

So white. White and cold.

A cold wall of white.

No. No.

I'm buried in it. Buried in the white.

Falling deeper, deeper . . .

I realized I was screaming now.

Not a scream of fun. Not a scream of delight.

I screamed in horror.

Screamed out pure terror.

Screamed until I felt my lungs about to burst.

And still I screamed.

Screamed so hard. Screamed so loud.

And the walls of white closed in.

As I screamed. Screamed. Screamed out my horror.

I knew I couldn't stop.

I knew I'd never stop.

chapter

11

I don't remember exactly how I got home.

Of course, Adriana and Laura must have helped me.

I can still see their troubled faces as they ran to pull me off my sled at the bottom of the hill. They had to pry my hands off the edge, then pull me to my feet.

I can see their wide eyes, their red cheeks. They were frantically talking to me. Shouting at me.

But I couldn't hear them. I was screaming too loud.

Screaming my throat raw.

Screaming. Screaming.

I saw the puzzled faces of the kids all around. I

saw a woman pull two little girls away. The girls were covering their ears with mittened hands, trying to shut out the shrill screams.

I saw them all. Saw their alarm. Saw their fear.

But I couldn't stop.

I couldn't control myself. I felt as if a creature inside me was struggling to burst out. Screaming and screaming—and forcing its way out of me.

What triggered my horror?

The snow? The sled? The feeling of sliding down, down, down so fast?

The feeling of being out of control?

Or was it the whirring walls of sparkling white snow?

What drove me over the edge like that?

I think I screamed all the way home.

I don't really remember. I don't remember returning home. And I don't remember finally closing my mouth, shutting off the horrible shrieks.

My throat felt raw. It burned as if on fire.

I couldn't speak. I could only whisper.

Martha, you're a total mess, I told myself.

Where was I?

Lying in my bed. The quilt pulled up to my chin.

Mom and Dad downstairs, making me a cup of tea. A bowl of hot soup. Dad on the phone, trying to reach Dr. Sayles.

I'm still shaking. My whole body shuddering. My throat throbbing and aching from my screams.

Lying in bed, staring up at the white ceiling.

The bright white ceiling.

And I had another flashback. Another picture slid into my mind, as rapidly as a sled racing downhill.

Another memory.

Of white. The cabins covered with snow. Powdery drifts up to the windows. Silvery icicles, stabbing down from the rain gutter like dagger blades.

I saw Justine. Laura. And then Adriana.

A snowball fight.

I heard a *thwock*. The sound of a snowball hitting the back of Adriana's parka.

I heard laughter. Boys' laughter.

More snowballs flew.

Then I saw Aaron beside me. Brown hair tumbling down from a brown-and-white-checked cap. A grin on his face. Cheeks red from the cold. Steam rising up from his open mouth.

Another *thwock*.

I felt myself duck as a snowball whirred close overhead.

Everyone was laughing. Shouting. Having such a good time.

Lying in bed, my eyes shut, I could feel myself smiling. It seemed like so much fun.

The snow sparkled. Aaron tossed a snowball at Laura. She ducked and dropped to her knees in the deep snow. A snowball hit her in the head, knocked her ski cap off.

Laughing, she scrambled to make fresh snow-balls. "I'll get you!" she was screaming at someone, pretending to be angry. "I'll get you!"

Who was she screaming at?

I struggled to see.

Aaron?

No. Ivan.

Ivan was there with us. In his leather jacket. No hat or gloves.

I saw his leering grin. Saw the small goatee under his chin.

Thwock. Another snowball caught Laura smack on the chest.

She laughed. Grabbed Ivan by the jacket collar. Struggled to pull him down into the deep snow.

Everyone laughing.

Everyone having so much fun.

I could see clearly now. I was remembering. My memory—this was a piece of it—coming back to me.

Ow!

I felt a shock of cold. Saw myself in the scene. Saw myself wiping a wet clump of snow off my forehead.

Heard laughter. Cold laughter.

Felt another snowball, hard and icy, smack just under my jacket collar.

Who was throwing them? Who was attacking me?

I squinted harder, trying to see the whole scene. Trying to remember, to bring it all back.

And saw Justine. Such an angry expression knotting her face.

Justine, pelting me with snowballs. Forming them furiously between her green gloves. Then heaving them. Heaving snowballs at me as fast as she could.

"Justine—!" I saw myself calling to her. "Hey— whoa!"

Justine ignored me. Threw even more furiously, letting out short grunts with each toss. Throwing as hard as she could.

Trying to hurt me?

Why is Justine angry at me? I wondered. Why is she picking on me?

And then I saw myself fight back. Saw myself fling snowballs back at her. Scooping up handful after handful of snow. Squeezing it hard. Heaving it before it was even shaped into snowballs.

The two of us crying out, shouting now. Heaping snow on each other. Both of us moving frantically, furiously.

The shouts all angry now.

Our expressions angry, too.

And then, feeling hands tugging me back. Seeing Ivan and Aaron, pulling me away. Seeing Laura and Adriana stepping in front of Justine.

Hearing Justine's angry shouts. But I can't understand her words.

What is she shouting about? Why is she so angry at me?

Laura and Adriana having to hold on to her,

having to pull her to the cabin. While Aaron and Ivan are grabbing my shoulders, trying to keep me still.

All that happiness. Everyone so cheerful. It disappeared so quickly. And I felt as cold as the snowy wind.

The white fades. The scene darkens.

What is happening?

Lying in bed, I struggle to keep the picture bright. To keep the scene alive.

I want to see more. I want to remember. I *need* to remember.

Darker now. And later. I am inside a cabin. I see a fire dancing in the fireplace across the room.

I am back against a wall. In deep shadows.

I struggle to see through the shadows. I am sitting on a long, low bench. My back against the wall.

Someone leans against me. Someone sits next to me.

It's so dark back here. As if we're hiding.

I struggle to see his face as he kisses me.

It's Aaron. It has to be Aaron, I know.

Who else would I be kissing back here in the shadows, away from all the others?

Aaron.

I kiss him again.

It's so dark. I still can't see his face.

Aaron—why can't I see you?

Because it isn't Aaron.

I feel a strong shudder as I struggle to remember.

THE FACE

And see the boy lean forward in the darkness and press his mouth against mine.

I feel his lips. Pushing. Pushing against my lips. So hard. So insistent.

And it isn't Aaron.

I'm kissing another boy.

Not Aaron. But who?

He pulls back. Smiles at me.

And I see his dark, serious eyes.

See the turned-up nose. The tiny white scar across the dark eyebrow.

I'm kissing him. Kissing him in the shadows.

I see him clearly now.

I see his face.

The face I've been drawing again and again.

chapter

12

The next afternoon I gathered up my drawings of the boy. I shoved them into my backpack. And I sneaked out of the house.

Aaron, you've got to help me, I pleaded silently. My boots sank through the hard crust on the snow as I walked quickly to his house. I pulled my parka tighter, leaning into a steady, cold wind.

Mom and Dad wanted me to stay in bed another day. They hadn't been able to reach Dr. Sayles. He was out of town at a conference. They wanted to keep me home safe and sound.

But I didn't feel safe and sound, even in my own bed with the quilt pulled up to my chin. Hot soup and cups of tea wouldn't calm me, wouldn't help me to rest.

Only knowing the truth will help, I decided.

Only knowing what happened last November will help to calm me down.

And Aaron can tell me. Aaron can help me.

A strong gust of frozen wind blew open my parka. I pulled it closed. Shifted the backpack on my back. Leaned forward as I trudged over the deep, crusty snow.

Aaron's house came into view in the next block. Two tall evergreens, covered in white snow, stood guard over the driveway. The driveway and front walk had been shoveled, the snow piled up on the sloping lawn. A single icicle, thick as a carrot, hung down over the front storm door.

I tried to push the doorbell, but it felt frozen. Stuck. I jabbed my finger against it again. No bell ringing inside the house.

So I knocked. I had rushed out of the house without any gloves. My frozen hand ached as I pounded three times on the door. Then three more times.

I could see lights on inside. I heard a cough. Then footsteps.

Aaron's little brother Jake pulled open the door.

"Hi," I said, my hand still raised, ready to knock again. "Is Aaron home?"

"Yeah. Sure." Jake stared up at me. He had a Kit Kat bar in one hand. He didn't move out of the way or invite me in.

"Well, can I see him?" I asked impatiently.

Aaron appeared before Jake could answer. He

shoved Jake out of the way. Jake shoved him back, then disappeared.

"Martha—hi!" Aaron brushed back his brown hair with one hand. He was wearing baggy jeans and a maroon-and-gray Shadyside High sweatshirt. "I didn't expect—"

"I have to talk to you!" I blurted out. I didn't mean to sound so excited. So desperate. But I suddenly couldn't catch my breath.

"I want to show you something, Aaron. I want you to tell me some things. I need some answers."

"Well . . ." He glanced back into the house. He frowned. He seemed tense.

What's his problem? I wondered, studying his face.

First Jake won't let me in. Now Aaron is making me stand out here in the cold.

"Can I come in?" I asked finally.

"Oh. Yeah. Sure." His cheeks turned pink. He stepped back.

I stamped my boots on the welcome mat and stepped into the warmth of the house. I could feel the cold follow me in. I pulled off the backpack, then the parka and tossed them onto the floor beside the living room couch.

"I'm just here watching Jake," Aaron offered.

"Your parents aren't home?"

He shook his head.

"I had to see you," I said.

"I—I heard about yesterday," Aaron stammered. He shoved his hands into his jeans pockets and turned his blue eyes to the front window. "I'm sorry. I . . ." His voice trailed off.

He's never this tense around me, I thought. What is his problem?

I rubbed my hands, trying to warm them. I could hear a TV on down the hall. Funny voices. A cartoon show. I heard Jake laughing.

"Aaron—" I started. "I want to show you these drawings I made." I bent down, reaching for the backpack—and heard a crash in the kitchen.

He gasped.

I stood up. "Is someone else here?"

His face reddened. "No. I—"

I crossed the room quickly. Made my way down the short hallway. Pushed open the kitchen door.

"Justine—!" I cried. "What are *you* doing here?"

chapter 13

Justine stood hunched over the sink, picking up pieces of the glass she had just dropped. I saw a puddle of spilled water on the floor.

She spun around as I burst in, and her mouth dropped open as if she wanted to scream.

"Justine came over to borrow my graphing calculator," Aaron explained, stepping up behind me. "The batteries wore down on hers."

"That's right," Justine agreed quickly. She pushed a tangle of red hair off her forehead. And turned to Aaron. "I'm sorry. I was getting a glass of water. I dropped it, and—"

"But you were *hiding* back here!" I exclaimed. My voice came out shrill and angry. "Justine— why were you hiding in the kitchen?"

"I—I wasn't!" she insisted. "Martha, really—
I—"

"I told her to," Aaron broke in. He stepped
between us. He scratched his wavy, brown hair
tensely with one hand and kept gazing from Justine
to me.

"You what?" I demanded.

"I told her to wait in the kitchen," Aaron explained. "I thought you would get the wrong idea."

"Excuse me?" I cried.

Justine dropped a jagged shard of glass onto the
counter. "Calm down, Martha. Everything is
okay," she said softly.

Aaron stepped up close behind me and put his
hands on my shoulders. "Yeah. Everything is
okay," he echoed.

"We both heard about yesterday," Justine said.
"We heard about how you lost it on Miller Hill.
When you knocked on the door, we saw you
through the front window. Aaron said I should go
in the kitchen. We didn't want to get you upset
again or anything."

Aaron turned me around. His blue eyes burned
into mine. "It was stupid. I'm sorry, Martha. It was
totally dumb. But I did it for you."

"We didn't want you to get upset again," Justine
added. "I just stopped by for the calculator. That's
the truth."

I lowered my eyes to the floor. The black and
gray dots on the linoleum flashed and shimmered. I

shut my eyes. "Sorry," I murmured. "I didn't mean to sound so suspicious. So . . . crazy."

Aaron slid his arm around my waist. Justine said some more comforting things. Aaron gave her the graphing calculator. She apologized again. Then she pulled on her coat and hurried out the front door.

I watched her through the living room window. She strode quickly down the driveway, her head lowered, biting her bottom lip. As I watched her, I tried to decide whether to believe them or not.

Aaron had been so great this whole time. He'd been so wonderful to me. So caring.

I decided I *had* to believe them.

I could feel Aaron's eyes on me. I turned to find him on the couch, tapping his fingers on the arm.

I hurried over and sat down at the other end of the couch.

"Sorry about the . . . mix-up," he murmured, tapping the couch arm a little faster.

"My memory is slowly coming back," I told him.

I could see the surprise on his face. Saw his jaw twitch. He swallowed.

"I keep seeing pictures," I continued. "Whole scenes. It's all coming back to me, bit by bit."

He sighed. Then he spoke in a soft, hushed tone just above a whisper. "When it does come back, it'll be hard for you."

He took my hand and squeezed it. I wanted him to keep holding it. But he quickly let go.

"What do you mean?" I demanded. "Why will it be hard for me?"

He hesitated. "You know I can't tell you that," he said, still in a whisper.

"Tell me," I insisted. "Why will it be hard for me?"

"The doctor told us not to help you," Aaron replied. He cleared his throat. "He told us that you had to get your memory back on your own. He made us promise not to tell you what happened that night."

"But, Aaron—" I grabbed his arm. I tried to pull him close, but he kept his place on the other end of the couch. "Why will it be so hard for me when I get back my memory?" I demanded again. "Why will I be so upset?"

He uttered a hoarse cry. His blue eyes locked on mine. "Because—something terrible happened!" he cried. "Something terrible, Martha."

He took a deep breath. His eyes remained on mine. "It changed us all." A strange smile crossed his face. A bitter smile. A smile I had never seen there before. "In a way, you're lucky you don't remember," he muttered.

"But, Aaron—"

His strange smile faded. He scratched his dark hair.

I let out a frustrated cry. I wanted him to tell me the whole story. Everything. But I knew he wouldn't. My friends were all being so good. All cooperating with Dr. Sayles.

The drawings.

How could I have forgotten about the drawings?

I reached over the couch and lifted my backpack. I struggled with the zipper. My hands were shaking. I pulled out the drawings.

"What are those?" Aaron demanded. He finally slid closer to me.

I held two of them up. "I've been drawing this face. Again and again."

His eyes bulged. He gasped.

"Who is it?" I demanded.

He shook his head. "No." Was that shock in his eyes? Was it fear?

"Tell me," I insisted. "I can't stop drawing this face. Tell me who it is, Aaron."

"No. No way," he replied, shaking his head.

I shoved the drawings into his face. "Tell me! Tell me! Tell me!"

He pushed them away. And jumped to his feet. "I can't, Martha. You know what the doctor said. You know that I can't tell you."

I jumped up beside Aaron. I wasn't going to let him get away. I wasn't going to give up.

The boy's face was driving me crazy.

I saw it everywhere I went. I couldn't erase it from my mind.

"Is he someone I know?" I demanded.

Aaron crossed his arms in front of him.

"Is he?" I repeated. I waved the drawings in Aaron's face.

He backed away. He made a zipper motion over

80

his mouth. "Stop it, Martha. I can't tell you. Stop making it hard for both of us. You know I can't say anything."

I could feel my chest tighten, my temples throb. I had to know. I had to know *now*.

"Do I know him, Aaron? Where is he? If I know him, why haven't I seen him in school? Why haven't I seen him?" I shrieked.

I guess I'd gone too far.

I could see Aaron start to lose it.

He balled his hands into fists. His face reddened. He gritted his teeth. Then he spit out an answer. "Know why you haven't seen him, Martha? Know why you haven't seen him?"

"Why?" I demanded. "Why?"

"Because he's dead!"

chapter 14

Tuesday night I finished my homework early. I sat down at my desk and opened my drawing pad.

A drawing of the dead boy's face slid out.

I held it between my hands, studying it.

Why am I drawing a dead boy? I asked myself.

I tilted the paper at one angle, then another. As if seeing it in a different way would bring me an answer.

The dark eyes stared out at me, revealing nothing.

Why am I drawing a dead boy?

Who is he?

Aaron refused to tell me any more about the boy.

He was furious at himself for losing control, for blurting out that the boy was dead.

I tried to apologize to Aaron in school. But he turned and hurried away. Whenever I called his house, Jake answered and said that Aaron wasn't home.

"I can't lose you, Aaron," I murmured out loud. "You mean too much to me. I can't lose you."

I stared at the face in the drawing. "Who are you?" I asked it. "And why was I kissing you in the cabin?"

Why was I drawing a dead boy? Why do I draw you over and over?

A frightening thought made me shiver despite the heat of my bedroom.

Was the dead boy controlling my hand?

Was he forcing me to draw him? Guiding my hand *from the grave?*

I crumpled up the drawing. Then I pulled two charcoal pencils from the desk drawer. I leaned over the drawing pad and tried to steady my hands.

"I'll draw a kitten," I decided.

The deadline for the art portfolio was only two weeks away. If I didn't have some drawings to show, I wouldn't be accepted in the special course.

"I'll draw you, Rooney. Where are you?"

Of course the stupid cat wasn't around when I needed her.

I leaned over the pad and started to draw her from memory.

"Martha," my mother called. "Adriana is here."

I heard Adriana's footsteps in the hall.

"Hi. What's up?" I asked as she stepped into the room.

"Not much. How's it going?" she answered. She tugged off her wool muffler and blue down jacket and tossed them onto my bed. She pushed back her curly, black hair with both hands. "Whoa. It's cold out. You look great!"

"Yeah. I feel okay," I replied softly. I'd been apologizing to Laura and Adriana ever since the sledding incident on Saturday. I must have apologized at least two dozen times and told them I was feeling fine.

But they kept checking up on me. And they kept telling me how great I looked all the time.

Adriana dropped down beside her jacket on my bed. She let out a long sigh. "You finish your homework?"

I nodded. "Yeah. I didn't have much. I thought I'd try sketching. This portfolio—"

"Things are bad at my house," Adriana interrupted.

"Your parents?" I asked. "Are they fighting again? Do you need to sleep here tonight?"

A lot of times when her parents were battling, Adriana escaped by staying at my house. There were times when things were really bad that she just about moved in with my family for good.

"No, it's not my parents," Adriana said, kicking the toe of her boot against a spot on the carpet. "Dad moved out Sunday." She moaned. "Finally."

I didn't know what to say. I knew that Adriana was closer to her father than her mother. I didn't think she was as happy about him leaving as she pretended.

"It's Ivan," she said, fiddling with her long, blue wool muffler. "It's Ivan I'm worried about."

I turned in the desk chair to face her. I pulled the drawing pad into my lap and sketched as I talked to her. "What did Ivan do this time?"

Adriana hesitated. "I—I'm not sure. But I went into his room tonight. To ask him something. And he had a new tape player and a new Discman."

I stopped sketching. "So? Why is that so terrible, Adriana?"

She twisted the muffler around her wrist. Her dark eyes flared. "Where did Ivan get the money for those things?"

I thought about that, waiting for her to continue.

"I think he's been stealing," she said finally. "I mean, he's been hanging out with some really tough kids. A couple of them got suspended from Waynesbridge High. I think they set a bathroom on fire or something."

"Nice," I muttered, rolling my eyes.

"Well, Ivan has been hanging out with these guys all the time," Adriana continued. "He says they're great guys. They know how to have fun."

She tossed the muffler back onto the bed. She frowned. "And now all of a sudden Ivan has a Discman and a new tape player. He's been stealing.

I know he has. He's so mixed up, Martha. He's going to ruin his life. And I—I—"

I started to reply.

But I gazed down at my sketch—and let out a startled cry. "No! Oh, no!"

I hadn't drawn a cat. I had drawn the face again. *Can't I draw anything else?*

I felt Adriana's hand on my shoulder. I turned to see her staring down at the boy's face.

I saw her swallow hard. Saw her eyes narrow. Saw her grit her teeth.

"Want to go to the basketball game Friday night?" she asked, her hand still resting on the shoulder of my sweater.

"Huh?"

"The Shadyside game. Friday night," she said. "Want to go? You know. Have some fun? Try to forget about everything?"

I don't want to forget, I thought unhappily. I want to *remember*.

"Sure," I told her. "Great idea. Let's have some fun."

Laura came with Adriana and me to the game. Laura picked us up a little early. So first we cruised around town in Laura's Bonneville, with the radio cranked up all the way.

We sang at the top of our lungs and shouted out the window at boys on the street. Squealing around corners. Laughing and joking.

Acting like jerks. But we didn't care. It had been

such a cold, grim winter. We were determined to
have some fun.

We roared into the student parking lot at school
about ten minutes after the game had started. And
scrambled into the gym, greeted by the steady *thud*
of the basketball being dribbled on the hardwood
floor and the shouts of the crowd.

As we climbed the bleachers, searching for a seat,
I glanced up at the scoreboard: already eight-to-two
in favor of our opponents, the Ironton Hawks. Not
a good start.

"Go, Tigers!" I shouted. "Tigers rule!"

Laura, Adriana, and I made some kids move
down. And we squeezed into seats near the top of
the bleachers.

Shadyside scored on an easy layup, and the
crowd sent up a cheer.

"Where's Aaron tonight?" Laura shouted over
the roar.

I shrugged. "Don't know. He didn't call." I
turned to the floor, determined to concentrate on
the game.

I wasn't going to worry about Aaron tonight. Or
anyone else.

I wanted to enjoy the basketball game. Cheer
with the crowd. Shout for the Tigers. Maybe cruise
around with Adriana and Laura after the game. Or
hang out at The Corner or Pete's Pizza.

Act like everyone else. Not like some freak with a
chunk of her life missing. Some freak everyone felt
sorry for.

"Go, Tigers!"

The whistle blew. A time-out. I saw Corky Corcoran jump up and lead the cheerleader squad onto the floor.

"Check out that guy on the Hawks!" Adriana shouted. She pointed to their bench across the floor.

"Which one?" I squinted against the bright lights. "The tall one?"

She laughed. "They're all tall. The one with the curly black hair."

I squinted harder. "The one who can't figure out how to tie his sneakers?"

Adriana ignored my sarcasm. "I'm cheering for *him!*" she declared. "Wow!"

I shook my head. "Traitor."

The cheerleaders did their splits, then went running off the floor. The players tossed down their towels and water bottles and walked back onto the floor.

A buzzer sounded. The game started up.

A close game. As it neared the half, the score was tied at twenty-four.

"I'm starving," Laura moaned. She tugged my arm. "Let's beat the crowd to the food counter."

"Yeah. Let's go," Adriana agreed.

With about a minute left in the half, the three of us started down the aisle of the bleachers. Outside the gym, food stands were set up with popcorn and hot dogs and stuff.

We were nearly down to the floor when a Hawks

player scored on a slam dunk. The crowd grumbled as the Hawks took the lead.

I saw our players turn to take the ball down the floor. Saw their faces set, their hard expressions. Eager not to be down at the half.

A pass. Then another pass.

The player started to dribble. Lost the ball. I saw the angry scowl on his face.

Saw his face.

His face.

No!

He had the face—the face in my drawing!

"It's *him!*" I shrieked, grabbing for Adriana. "It's him! It's him!"

I missed her shoulder. Started to fall down the bleacher aisle.

Caught my balance. Raised my eyes to the floor.

Another Shadyside player turned. He had the face too!

I stared at two more players.

Stared at their wavy, brown hair. Their turned-up noses. Their serious, dark eyes.

The face!

They all had the face! The face I'd been drawing.

The face of the dead boy.

And as they turned to stare back at me, their smiles faded. Their mouths twisted. Eyes bulged in horror.

They all started to scream.

And I screamed with them.

chapter

15

"It's him! It's the dead boy! It's him!"

Was that *me* shouting those words over and over?

I could feel everyone's eyes on me as Adriana and Laura pulled me from the bleachers.

"It's him! Let me go! The dead boy! The dead boy! I have to see him!"

The buzzer went off right over our heads. It shocked me into silence.

My friends dragged me to the gym doors. I struggled free. I had to see him. Had to talk to him.

But the players had all turned away. They were running off the floor to the locker room.

"Martha—come on!" Adriana pulled me out

into the hall. She and Laura led me away from the food stands. Down the long hallway.

We stopped at the stairs beside the darkened cafeteria.

"I'll get her something to drink," Laura told Adriana. I watched her run back toward the gym.

I sat down on the bottom step. Adriana dropped down beside me. "Martha—are you okay now?"

"I—I don't know," I replied honestly.

I shut my eyes and saw the players again. The players with the same face. His face.

"Am I okay? I really don't know, Adriana."

When I opened my eyes, she had a large silvery coin in her hand. "Let me show you a relaxation exercise I learned from Dr. Corben. It always calms me down when I'm stressed."

She held the coin up close to my face. "Watch the coin," she whispered. "Follow it with your eyes."

She moved the coin slowly, left and right, close to my face. It glimmered dully in the dim light. Adriana whispered softly as I followed the coin. "Concentrate on the coin. Calm. Calm. Just watch the coin."

Eager for the faces to disappear, I obeyed.

I wanted to be calm. I wanted to be okay.

The coin floated slowly in front of me. Back and forth. Back and forth.

I grabbed Adriana's hand. "Whoa. What are you doing?"

"It's okay, Martha," she replied softly. She gently removed my hand from her wrist. "I'm giving you a hypnotic suggestion. To calm you down."

I narrowed my eyes at her. Her face disappeared into shadow, then came back into view as she leaned close. "You're . . . hypnotizing me?" I demanded.

She nodded. Her black hair fell over her eyes. "Relax. I do it to myself all the time. It's easy."

She raised the coin again, but I brushed her hand aside. "I'm feeling better," I told her.

Laura hurried up to us. She handed me a paper cup of cold water. She studied me as I took the cup from her, her face filled with concern. "You okay?"

I nodded. Took a long sip of the cold water. "Yeah. I'm fine. Really. I—I don't know what happened in there."

I heard shouts from the gym. Loud laughter in the hall.

I wanted to be laughing too. I didn't want to be sitting here in the dark, sipping water, staring into my friends' worried faces.

"What happened?" Laura demanded.

I shook my head. I tilted the cup and finished the water. "I don't know. I saw the face. You know. The face I've been drawing. The Tigers—the whole team—they all had the same face."

I saw Laura exchange glances with Adriana.

"Pretty weird," Adriana muttered.

I took a deep breath. "Whose face is it?" I demanded. I jumped up from the step and grabbed

92

Laura by the shoulders. "Tell me! Tell me right now. Whose face is it?"

Adriana gently pulled me away from Laura. "You know we can't do that," she said, softly but firmly.

Laura lowered her eyes. "I wish I could help you, Martha. But your doctor said—"

"Tell me!" I screamed. "Tell me!"

"Let's get you home," Laura said softly.

They started to guide me to the doors.

My legs felt shaky and weak. My whole body felt tense and trembly.

People were standing around outside the gym, eating and talking. Some kids called to us, but we kept walking.

I tried not to look at anyone. I was afraid. Afraid I'd see the boy's face again.

We passed the gym and turned the corner, making our way to the back door that led to the parking lot. The air turned cooler. I could hear the buzzer in the gym. The second half was about to begin.

I suddenly felt so terrible.

I just wanted to have a good time. And now I'd spoiled the whole evening. For myself and for my two friends.

I opened my mouth to apologize when I saw someone against the lockers at the far wall. A boy and a girl. Hidden in shadows, they had their arms wrapped around each other. The girl had her back against the lockers. The boy was kissing her.

Kissing her.

His back turned to us.

He pulled his head back and turned slowly as the three of us started to pass by. I guess he heard our footsteps on the floor.

He turned and his face came into view.

His face.

I saw his face.

I didn't want to believe it.

But I saw him so clearly.

Saw his face so clearly.

"No!" I cried. "It's you! No!"

chapter

16

"Martha—wait!" he called. He spun away from the girl against the locker.

"Aaron—!" I choked out.

And as he came toward me, I saw the girl. Saw the tangle of red hair. The pale, round face. The bright red lipstick, smeared from kissing.

Justine.

Her lipstick smeared from kissing Aaron.

Aaron and Justine.

"Martha—listen," Aaron started, breathing hard.

From kissing her? Or from the surprise of seeing me?

He took a deep breath and started again. "Martha—I have to tell you—"

Adriana shoved him back. "Not now, Aaron," she said sharply.

"Martha is having a tough time," Laura told him. She tugged me away.

"Go away, Aaron," Adriana said coldly. "You too, Justine. Just go away. No way Martha wants to talk to you now."

She and Laura pulled me away.

I saw Aaron give a helpless shrug. I tried to read his expression, but I couldn't figure it out.

Did he look guilty? Embarrassed?

Didn't he care?

I saw him and Justine turn and head to the gym.

Then, suddenly, I was out the door. Into the dark night.

The darkest night.

My darkest night.

Plunged into such cold darkness. Because I believed in Aaron. I believed he cared about me.

Not Justine. Not Aaron and Justine.

Now what could I believe in?

What?

I can't even believe in my own mind! I realized.

Such a dark night of hallucinations, of unreal faces—and real faces.

Aaron and Justine. Why couldn't they be a hallucination too?

Why were they kissing in the hall when I believed in them?

What can I believe now?

Before I realized it, Laura and Adriana were gone. I was back in my bedroom. Back in the light.

Staring into the harsh white light of my desk lamp. Sitting there, sketching again. Drawing the boy's face. Staring into the bright light as if being warmed by it. Calmed by it.

I never wanted to see the darkness again.

I wanted to stay in the light. Swim in it. Bathe in it. Live in it.

And draw the face. Draw it again and again.

And as I stared into the light, the face began to move.

It moved in my memory. Another scene, a lost scene from that forgotten November.

My memory started to return.

I stared into the light, willing the memory back, willing it to life.

Will it *all* come back this time? I wondered.

Will I get it *all* this time? I asked myself, gazing into the warm, white light, filled with eagerness—and cold dread.

chapter

17

"Don't push me like that," I whispered.

He grinned at me, his face so close, so close I could smell the chocolate on his breath. "You like it," he insisted.

"No." I tried to shove him back. He had his arm around my shoulder. He pressed against me. "No. I don't like it. Really."

That made him laugh.

He pressed closer. Lowered his head and kissed me.

I tasted the chocolate now. He'd been eating a candy bar. He pressed his lips harder against mine. Too hard.

I tried to back away, but he was holding on to me so tightly.

I couldn't breathe!

I heard the others in the other room of the cabin. Heard something crackle loudly in the fireplace. Heard Justine's high laugh.

Why wasn't I with them? Why wasn't I with my friends?

Why was I in the dark back room of this cabin, kissing this strange boy when I should be with my friends?

Where was Aaron?

Why wasn't I kissing Aaron?

I listened for his voice in the other room. Heard Ivan instead. Heard Ivan say, "Throw another log on. Hey, somebody—throw another log on before it dies down."

Heard Adriana tell her brother, "You do it. Don't just sit there ordering us around."

I wanted to get up. Join them. See the fire. Be with Aaron. I was still going with Aaron. I should be with him now.

But the boy held on to me, held me so tightly.

And kissed me again. Rubbing his face roughly against mine.

Hurting me.

"No. Sean—please."

His name is Sean?

Sean?

Sean?

I know his name.

Staring into the white desk light, I struggled to see more. I knew the boy's name. But I needed to see the rest.

What happens next? I asked myself.

I know your name, Sean. But who are you? Why am I sitting in the dark with you? Why am I kissing you?

What happens next?

I stared into the light, struggling to see more. Struggling to see everything.

And I saw myself shove Sean hard. He reacted with an angry cry.

He shoved me back.

We jumped to our feet. I could still taste the chocolate on my mouth, the chocolate of his rough kisses.

But now we were fighting. Shoving each other. Shouting.

I couldn't hear the words.

I could feel my anger. More than anger. I felt *rage*.

I shoved him in the chest. I slapped him.

Oh!

The sound of that slap.

But why were we fighting?

Why?

With a trembling hand, I clicked off the desk light. I didn't want to see any more. It was too upsetting.

My whole body shook. The back of my neck felt cold and damp.

The memory had been so sharp, so painfully clear. I wasn't just remembering that night—I was *reliving* it.

I started to pull myself to my feet. But a blinking red light caught my attention. I stared down at my answering machine. The blinking light meant that I had a message.

Had it been blinking the whole night?

I pushed the button and listened to the squeal of the tape rewinding.

A few seconds later the message began to play. I heard crackling. A lot of background noise. Like from a restaurant or a crowded room.

And then a girl's voice, harsh, raspy. A girl's whispered voice: *"You keep drawing him because you killed him."*

"Huh?" I let out a startled cry.

Leaned closer, listening for the rest.

But the caller hung up. A click. Then silence.

The tape rewound itself.

I pushed the button. Listened to it again, gripping the edges of my desk.

"You keep drawing him because you killed him."

"Nooo!" I wailed. "Laura—is that you? Laura?"

It sounded like Laura, making her voice low and raspy. Laura disguising her voice.

"Is it you, Laura? What do you mean?"

I pushed the button and played the message again. And again. And again.

"You keep drawing him because you killed him."

No. No, I told myself.

It can't be true. It can't be.

Laura—was that you? Did you leave that horrifying message?

Why are you doing this to me?

chapter

18

"Please come in." Dr. Corben held open the door to her inner office, and I followed her inside.

She was a short, gray-haired woman. Tiny with delicate, doll-like features. She wore a black pant-suit that fit her perfectly. She could have been anywhere between forty and sixty. I really couldn't tell.

Her office was small and dark. Every surface was cluttered with piles of books, thick folders, stacks of magazines, and papers.

She had no nurse or receptionist. She was all alone here. In this dark, cluttered office. Such a serious room. The Garfield the Cat cookie jar on her desk seemed totally out of place.

I felt the blood start to throb at my temples. I suddenly felt really tense.

I should turn around and leave, I told myself.

But no. I felt so desperate now. So frightened after that ugly phone message. I had to find out the truth. All of it. I had to know.

The doctor's warm smile reassured me. "Take a seat, Martha." She motioned to the wooden chair in front of her desk. "It's cold in here, isn't it?"

I nodded. "A little. It's very windy out."

"I've been fighting with the landlord about the heat," she said, lowering herself into her desk chair and shoving a stack of files aside. "Do you need a sweater or anything?"

I was wearing a big, long-sleeved T-shirt over black tights. "No. I'm fine. Really." I crossed my legs, then uncrossed them. I felt so uncomfortable.

"How can I help you?" Dr. Corben asked, smiling again.

"I . . . well . . ." I took a deep breath and started again. "I'm interested in hypnosis, Dr. Corben. I know it's your specialty. I mean, you hypnotize people—right?"

She slid open her center desk drawer and pulled out a long yellow pad. She set it down on the desktop in front of her but didn't write anything. "Hypnosis is a tool that I use," she replied. She brushed a strand of gray hair off her forehead.

"And hypnosis can be used to help people get back their memory—right?" I asked, squeezing the wooden chair arms.

She nodded. Then she raised her tiny gray-blue eyes to mine. "Do you have memory loss, Martha?"

"Well . . . yes." I sighed. "Something happened last November. Some kind of accident. I haven't been able to remember it. Just pieces of it."

I crossed my legs again. My heart was suddenly pounding. "I really want to know what happened to me, Dr. Corben. Can you hypnotize me? Can you hypnotize me and bring back my memory?"

She gripped the yellow pad with both hands, sliding her hands up and down the sides of it. "You've had memory loss since last November?"

I nodded.

She narrowed her eyes and leaned across the desk. "You are under a doctor's care—right?"

I nodded again. "Yes, but—"

She raised a hand to stop me. "Did you bring a note from your doctor? Any instructions?"

"No. I didn't tell him," I blurted out.

Dr. Corben sank back into the desk chair. "Well, I could telephone your doctor, I suppose. You see, I cannot proceed until I have spoken with him and learned all the details. It wouldn't be right. In fact, it could be quite damaging."

"No. Please—" I started. I knew that Dr. Sayles wouldn't approve of this. I knew he'd be upset that I came here without telling him.

Dr. Corben tapped a pencil against the yellow pad. "How did you find out about me, Martha? How did you know to come here?"

"My friend Adriana," I told her. "Adriana Petrakis?"

"Oh, yes. Of course." Dr. Corben smiled again. "She was having trouble sleeping."

"And you really helped her," I said breathlessly. "She told me how you showed her how to hypnotize herself. It helped her a lot. And the other night, I had some trouble at the basketball game. And Adriana hypnotized me, and she—"

"She *what?*" Dr. Corben jumped to her feet, her face tight with shock. "Adriana did v. *hat?*"

"She used a coin. She gave me a hypnotic suggestion. To calm me down. I think it worked because—"

"She has no business doing that!" Dr. Corben exclaimed. "That is so dangerous, Martha. Adriana doesn't have the skill or the knowledge. She doesn't know what she's playing with. You must never let her try that on you again."

"I—I'm sorry," I murmured, swallowing hard.

Oh, no, I thought, feeling my stomach tighten with dread. Now I've gotten Adriana into major trouble.

"She was just trying to help me," I offered. "Actually, I think it *did* help me."

Dr. Corben didn't seem to hear me. "I'll have to call her," she said fretfully. "I'll have to speak to Adriana. And her parents."

I uttered a frustrated groan. "But what about me?" I blurted out in a high, shrill voice. "Will you hypnotize me? Will you help me get my memory back?"

Dr. Corben shook her head. She fixed a sympathetic stare on me. "I'd like to help, Martha," she said softly. "But I need to talk to your doctor first. And your parents. I need their permission before I can—"

I didn't wait for her to finish. I leaped up from the chair—so hard, I sent it toppling to the floor. As it clattered onto its back, I turned and ran.

Out of the dingy, cluttered office. Through the tiny, dark waiting room. Out the front door of the rundown building.

Dark clouds hovered low in the sky. The air felt heavy and wet.

I sucked in mouthfuls of the cold air. Then, as I started to my car, a figure stepped away from the wall.

"Martha—wait!" he called.

I froze as he stepped out of the shadows.

"Sean!"

My knees started to buckle.

I felt myself lose my balance, start to collapse to the pavement.

He hurried across the parking lot.

Sean?

No. Not Sean.

Aaron.

"Aaron—what are you doing here?" I choked out.

He wore a brown leather bomber jacket over a black flannel shirt. The jacket flapped open as he ran to catch up to me. His dark hair flew around his head.

"Martha, whoa." He stopped in front of me, his breath trailing up over his head. He brushed back his hair with both hands. "I want to explain," he said breathlessly.

I could feel my throat tighten. Once again, maybe for the thousandth time, I pictured him in the dark hall at school, kissing Justine. Kissing my friend.

Aaron and Justine.

I eyed him coldly. I realized in that instant that I didn't feel the same way about Aaron anymore.

I still cared about him. Maybe I even loved him.

But I didn't trust him.

"I want to explain," he repeated. He placed a hand on the shoulder of my jacket. But I stepped back, away from his hand.

"Well? Go ahead," I challenged him. I wanted to sound cold and hard. But my voice trembled.

"Justine and I are tired of sneaking around," Aaron said, his dark eyes on mine. "In a way, I'm glad you saw us."

"You and Justine—?" I couldn't keep the hurt out of my voice. But his words cut through me, sharper than the cold wind.

He nodded. "Justine and I don't want to hurt you, Martha. But we've been going out. For several months."

"Is that why Justine and I got into that fight up at the cabins?" I demanded.

Aaron nodded. "Yes. You remember that?"

"Yes. I'm remembering things," I said coldly. "But, Aaron—you and I . . . ?" My voice trailed off. I didn't know what to say. I felt so much hurt. And my hurt was quickly giving way to anger.

"I'm really sorry," he murmured. He lowered his eyes. "We know you're still in shock. Since what happened."

I guess that's when I totally lost it. I grabbed his shoulders with both hands. I started shaking him. Hard. "What happened?" I demanded. "Tell me, Aaron. Tell me now. What happened? What happened to Sean?"

His mouth dropped open in shock. He grabbed my hands and held on to them, forced me to stop shaking him. "You—you remember Sean?" he stammered.

Aaron took a step back. He seemed to stagger, as if overcome with shock. "You remember Sean?"

I nodded, studying Aaron's startled expression.

Why does Aaron look so frightened? I found myself wondering. Why is he frightened that I'm starting to remember?

"Tell me what happened," I insisted. "Tell me *now*, Aaron."

"I—I can't," he stammered. He turned away from me. "It's too . . . horrible."

chapter 19

After school on Wednesday I heard shouts as I made my way to my locker.

I turned the corner and saw two boys wrestling, shoving each other in the middle of the hall. A crowd had gathered. Kids were screaming and cheering.

I heard an angry cry. One boy sprawled backward into a metal locker. The sound of the collision rose over the excited screams of the crowd.

As I jogged toward them, the boys grabbed each other. A hard punch made a head snap back.

Some kids screamed.

I saw a trickle of blood puddle the floor.

Gazing up, I saw Ivan.

Ivan throwing himself on a boy I didn't recognize.

Blood gushing down Ivan's chin, staining the front of his gray shirt.

"Ivan—stop!" I shrieked.

They were down on the floor now, grunting and shouting, punching each other. Ivan, red-faced, sweat drenching his forehead, grabbed the boy's throat with both hands.

I dove beside him. Reached for Ivan's shoulders, determined to pull him off, to pull him away.

He was choking the other boy. His hands tightening around the boy's throat.

Choking him. Choking him.

They rolled away from me.

"Ivan—stop!" I shrieked at the top of my lungs. "Stop!"

And then there were other hands tugging at the two fighters. Other voices. Harsh shouts.

I climbed to my feet and saw Mr. Hernandez, the principal, tugging Ivan away.

The other boy lay on his back, rubbing his neck, groaning. He had blood down the front of his denim shirt. Was it his blood? Or Ivan's?

I couldn't tell. I gazed at the blur of bodies, the excited faces. Two teachers were helping the boy to his feet. He groaned, and blood gushed from his open mouth, thickly down his chin.

"What was *that* about?" somebody behind me demanded.

"Ivan started it," I heard a girl mutter.

"Who was the other guy?"

"I don't think he's goes to Shadyside."

"Well, what were they fighting about?"

"Look. One of them lost a tooth."

"Yuck!"

I stepped away from the excited conversation. I really didn't want to hear it.

I felt so bad for Ivan.

I turned the corner and saw Mr. Hernandez pulling Ivan down the hall. Ivan had his head lowered, his black hair toppling down in front of his face.

Like a criminal, I thought.

My friend. Adriana's brother.

Being taken away like a criminal.

I sighed. "Ivan—what is your problem?"

The phone was ringing when I finally got home from school. I tossed down my backpack and hurried to answer it.

"Hello?" I said breathlessly, pulling off my coat with my free hand.

"Martha, it's me."

Laura.

"Did you hear about Ivan? He got suspended from school," Laura said, speaking rapidly, excitedly.

"I was there," I told her. I let my coat fall to the

floor and stepped away. "I saw the fight. It was a really bad one."

"I guess," Laura replied. I could picture her rolling her eyes. "Hernandez suspended Ivan for two weeks. His parents have to come in for a conference tomorrow."

"Wow," I murmured. "They're not going to be happy about this."

"What was the fight about?" Laura demanded.

I shifted the phone to my other hand and sat down on the floor, leaning against the wall. "I don't know. They were already killing each other when I showed up."

"The other boy was from Drake Academy," Laura informed me. "He doesn't even go to Shadyside. He's one of Ivan's friends from—"

"Some friend!" I interrupted. "They really were trying to kill each other."

Laura let out a long moan. "I can't believe I used to go out with Ivan. Thinking about it just gives me the creeps. He's such an animal. I'm so glad I broke up with him."

I had a flash of memory. So surprising, I nearly dropped the phone.

"Laura—" I said, swallowing. "You broke up with Ivan to go with Sean!"

I heard her gasp on the other end of the line. I waited for her to reply. But heard only silence.

"Laura—?" I urged her to answer me. The

memories were washing back, bright pictures sweeping into my mind.

"Martha—you remember Sean?" Laura finally said, in a tiny voice.

"You broke up with Ivan that week," I told her, shutting my eyes. Shutting my eyes and letting the pictures come back to me.

"Yes. I—" Laura started.

But I didn't let her finish. I didn't want to interrupt the flow of my memories.

"You broke up with Ivan at the cabins. He was so upset, he and Sean almost got into a big fight there."

"Yes. That's right." Laura's voice suddenly sounded cold. Distant. "I—I don't want to talk about it," she stammered.

"You *have* to talk about it!" I cried. "You have to tell me, Laura—"

"No—!" she insisted. "No. I don't. I can't. I have to go now, Martha."

"Wait!" I cried. "Did you call me the other night? Did you leave a phone message for me?"

"I have to go," Laura repeated. "Really."

"Laura—answer me!"

"Call me later," she said breathlessly. "I have to go. We'll talk later, okay? Bye."

The phone went dead. But I stood there with the receiver in my hand, staring at the wall. The white wall.

The memories were flooding back.

THE FACE

I shut my eyes and let them come back.

The pictures were so vivid, so clear. This time I was going to see everything.

I was going to remember it all.

All the fun.

All the trouble.

All the horror.

chapter

20

As Ivan pulled the sled toward the cabin, Sean did a bellyflop onto it. "Give me a ride, man," Sean called, grinning up at Ivan.

Ivan grinned back. "I'll give you a ride. Off the side of the mountain!" He dropped the sled rope. "Get off, Sean. No way I'm pulling you up the hill."

Sean laughed and rolled off the sled, into the deep snow. He grabbed two handfuls and heaved them at Ivan. "Think fast!"

I watched from a short distance down the hill. I pulled a sled behind me too, an old wooden Flexible Flyer. My legs ached. I had been sledding all afternoon.

We had all been sledding. Me and all of my friends.

Justine, Adriana, and Laura. Aaron, Ivan, and Sean.

Sean wasn't really part of the group. Well, I guess maybe he was the newest member.

Sean was Ivan's friend. Ivan had met him at a bowling alley or some place. Sean lived in the Old Village. But he didn't go to Shadyside High.

I liked Sean. I thought he was interesting looking, with his dark eyes, his serious expression, and the tiny white scar that cut across his eyebrow. The one flaw that kept him from being perfectly handsome.

"Stack the sleds against that wall," Adriana instructed us.

Adriana had been in charge for the whole long weekend. Her parents owned the two cabins we were all staying at. But her parents never used them.

Too busy fighting, I thought with some sadness.

So Adriana was in charge. They were Ivan's cabins too, of course. But Ivan wasn't the kind of guy to give instructions—or be helpful in any way.

Ivan only cared about sneaking off and being alone with Laura.

I dropped my sled beside the others. Aaron helped me stack it on top of the pile. He smiled at me. "That was awesome sledding!"

I started to reply. But he hurried away to join Justine and Laura.

"Skiing next!" someone shouted.

"Yeah. Let's hit the slopes!"

A narrow ski run dropped down beside the cabins.

Such luxury! I thought. To have your own private ski slope!

I glanced around. Justine and Adriana had opened the shed and were pulling out skis and ski poles and tossing them onto the snow. Ivan and Laura were head to head, arguing heatedly about something in front of the boys' cabin.

Aaron had disappeared into the cabin. Then Ivan and Sean were throwing snow at each other again beside their sled.

I took a deep breath. The air smelled so fresh and piney. The late afternoon sun still floated high in a cloudless blue sky.

"Come on—let's ski!" Adriana urged, calling everyone to the shed. "We want to go into town for dinner, right? It's getting late."

I gazed down the ski slope. Not very difficult, I decided. Not too steep. A straight path between two rows of tall fir trees.

Pretty easy, even for a beginner like me.

"Who's going first?" Laura called, hurrying away from Ivan.

I saw Aaron step out of the boys' cabin and come jogging across the snow. Aaron was an expert skier. This slope was baby stuff to him, I knew.

"We have to go one at a time," Adriana told us. "The slope is so narrow."

I turned to see Aaron dragging Ivan over to the skis. "We have a volunteer!" Aaron shouted.

Ivan scowled and angrily pulled away from Aaron. I saw Aaron react with surprise. Ivan spit in the snow and muttered something to Aaron.

"Hey—what's your problem?" Aaron asked Ivan.

Laura had walked over to Justine, and the two of them were talking, serious expressions on their faces.

"Who's going first?" someone asked.

"I think Martha goes first!" Adriana replied. She grinned at me and handed me a pair of skis.

"Why me?" I demanded.

"You were the champion sledder," Adriana declared.

A few kids cheered.

"You've won the first spot," Adriana continued.

"Are you kidding? I fell off my sled three times!" I exclaimed. "I nearly smashed into that tree!"

"I'm going second," Sean announced.

"Good. Then you can rescue me when I break my leg!" I told him.

I bent to fasten the skis. My heart started to pound. I had only skied two or three times before in my whole life. I really didn't have much confidence.

I knew I was about to make a total fool of myself in front of my friends.

I couldn't get the straps right. I turned and saw Adriana, and Justine, and a couple other kids watching me.

"Somebody else go first!" I shouted. "These straps are messed up."

"Okay. Here goes!" I heard Sean yell.

I fixed the straps. Pulled them tight. Then I stood up in time to watch Sean start his run.

I moved to the edge of the hill, the skis crunching in the crusty snow.

Sean pushed off with both poles and started down.

It was steeper than I thought. He bent forward and picked up speed. His skis slid over a bump. He kept his balance and swooped down faster.

And then up ahead of him, I saw the silver line.

A silver line across the ski run.

So slender. A glimmer. A glimmering thread against the white snow.

Shimmering in the sunlight, it cut straight across Sean's path.

I stared at it, puzzled. Trying to figure it out.

What was it?

It was as if someone had taken a silver pen and drawn a straight line across the ski run from tree to tree.

A silver line.

It took me so long to realize it was a wire.

It took me so long to realize that someone had strung a silver wire across the ski path.

It took me so long, there was no time to scream.

No time to warn Sean.

No time to move.

And a second later—maybe less—Sean skied into it.

The wire caught him at the throat.

Cut through his neck.

A straight line. A silver line.

It cut through his neck.

Bright red splashed on both sides of the silver line.

I still didn't move. I didn't believe it.

No one moved.

We all stood at the edge, staring down in silence.

The silver wire sliced off Sean's head.

I watched his body continue to ski. The skis carried it for several yards before it collapsed.

And Sean's head bounced onto the snow.

And emptied out. Emptied out. Emptied out.

Staring up at us.

Puddling the snow dark red.

chapter
21

I finally remembered. Remembered it all.

And now I stared down at my desk, cluttered with drawings of Sean. Stared down at his serious face.

And pictured his head, his handsome head, lying on the pure, white snow. His dark eyes staring up the slope at us, staring so accusingly.

I wrapped my arms around myself, trying to stop my body from shivering.

But the chills wouldn't stop. They rolled down my body. I felt so cold, so cold and frightened.

As if I were standing on the slope again. As if I were back in the snow, staring in horror at the thin silver line.

Helpless.

So helpless and horrified.

My memory was back. So sharp and clear, I felt sick all over again.

I wiped tears off my face with both hands. I hadn't even realized I was crying.

Now I let the sobs come. Sobs that tightened my face, tightened my throat until I gasped for breath.

Sean. Poor Sean.

And then I remembered even more.

I had a fight with Sean. An ugly fight.

I had a fight with Sean—and then he died.

The night before, Sean and I had fought.

And then he died. And the police came. I remembered their blue-black uniforms against the whiteness of the snow.

Remembered their stern faces, red from the cold. Eyes staring hard at me, studying me.

Remembered their questions. Endless questions.

They questioned us all. For hours and hours.

And then?

I still didn't remember.

But I remembered enough.

Aaron was right. I was better off before the horrible memory came back.

I hugged myself tighter, trying to force away the chills that shook my body.

And then the phone rang.

Adriana.

"I remember everything!" I blurted out. "Adriana, it all came back to me—just now!"

"Oh, I'm so sorry," she whispered. "It's so horrible, Martha. You must feel so bad."

"Yes," I admitted. I tried to say more, but the words caught in my throat.

"It's been so horrible. For all of us," Adriana murmured into the phone. "Ever since that day, we—"

"Adriana—that wire," I interrupted. "Did somebody deliberately plan to kill one of us?"

Silence. Then: "No one knows, Martha."

"Huh?" I cried. "But the police—? Didn't they figure out what happened?"

Adriana sighed. "It took forever for the police to get up the slope. We were all crying and screaming. We were all out of our minds. Poor Laura. They had to give her medication to put her to sleep. And Ivan nearly went nuts."

"But, the police—" I tried to say.

"They questioned us all. They studied the wire. Then they took it down and brought it to their lab. But they couldn't figure out who strung the wire. Or why."

Tears rolled down my cheeks. I made no attempt to brush them away. I was concentrating on Adriana's words, trying to understand what she was telling me.

And now I could hear her crying too. Short, gasping sobs. "I—I—I—" she stammered. "I don't know. It was so awful. Such a total nightmare, Martha."

Silence while she tried to get herself together.

Then she continued in a shaky voice. "I'll never get over it. I haven't slept since. Not a single night, Martha. Not a single night that I didn't live that nightmare again. Again and again."

"Adriana—" I started.

But she uttered a loud sob and kept talking. "I can't concentrate. I don't hear a word in school. I can't do my homework. My grades—my grades . . . I can't think straight."

A cold shudder nearly made me drop the phone. I gripped it tighter in my clammy hand. "Adriana," I choked out, "you don't think one of *us* killed Sean—do you?"

"What do *you* think?" she replied, shouting now. Screaming the words as if she were angry. "What do *you* think, Martha? There was no one else up on that hilltop. No one. We were the only ones up there. Who else could have strung that wire?"

The wire.

The silver wire.

I pictured the wire as I tried to digest Adriana's words.

Who else could have strung that wire?

No one else was up there. We were the only ones.

The only ones who could have killed Sean.

"I'm coming over," Adriana said suddenly, jarring me from my thoughts. Her voice was filled with emotion. "I'm coming over. I've been so worried about you, Martha. It must have been so horrible for you. Losing your memory. Then starting to draw Sean's face again and again."

"Yes. I—I didn't understand anything." I sighed. "It took me so long to put it together. It took me so long to remember."

A question forced its way into my mind, a question I didn't want to ask myself.

Why did I lose my memory? Why not one of the others, one of my friends?

Why did I take Sean's death so much harder than anyone else? Why did it affect me so strongly?

Was it because I had fought with Sean the night before he was murdered? Did I feel guilty because I had fought with him on his last night on earth?

Why? Why?

It was a question I couldn't answer.

But maybe someone could help answer it now. Maybe Adriana would help me now.

"Yes—please," I pleaded. "Come over. Come over right now."

"I'm on my way," she replied softly. And the phone went dead.

I set down the receiver, thinking hard. My mind whirring at top speed.

Remembering.

Who had a reason to kill Sean?

Who would want Sean dead?

Ivan? No. Sean was Ivan's friend. Ivan had brought him into our group.

Aaron? Laura? Justine?

No. No. Of course not.

Everyone liked Sean. Everyone.

I crossed my bedroom to the closet and pulled

open the door. I wanted to get changed before Adriana arrived.

I pulled a pair of faded jeans from the shelf in back.

I was glad Adriana had decided to come over. Maybe now we could have a long, long talk. Get everything off our chests.

I needed to talk. And I knew it would be good for Adriana.

The poor girl. She was so wrecked. She was having such a bad time of it. Her parents fighting the Battle of the Century. Her brother suspended from school, ruining his life.

I heard a car door slam out front.

Startled, I dropped the jeans.

I bent to pick them up off the closet floor.

And saw a brown bag. A brown canvas carry-all.

"Oh!" I uttered a short cry as I remembered it.

The bag I had taken on the trip up to the cabins. The bag I had packed all my stuff in last November.

What is it doing here in the back of my closet? I wondered. Did I forget to unpack it? Did I just shove it back here and forget about it?

I dragged it out into my room. My hands shook as I opened it.

The bag was nearly full. I pulled out wrinkled sweaters and rolled-up jeans. Two pairs of tights.

I never unpacked, I realized.

I must have been so upset, so out-of-my-mind, I just hid the bag away.

I pulled out more clothes. A cosmetics bag. My old hair dryer.

And then—

"Noooo!" I screamed out loud when I saw it. A high wail of horror.

At the bottom of the bag. Coiled up in a corner of the bag. Tucked tightly away.

Wire.

Silver wire.

Rolled-up tightly.

Beside a pair of wire cutters.

The wire that killed Sean?

I stared into the bag, afraid to move, afraid to look—unable to look away. I stared into the bag, stared at the coiled-up wire.

And I knew.

I knew who killed Sean.

I did.

I was the one.

"You've been drawing him because you killed him."

chapter

22

I heard the front door open. I heard Mom talking to Adriana downstairs.

But I didn't move.

I stared into the bag, stared at the silver wire.

One word repeated in my mind: Why? Why? Why?

It drowned out the voices downstairs. Drowned out the pounding thuds of my heartbeats, my shrill, gasping breaths.

Why? Why? Why?

Why did I kill Sean?

I shut my eyes and struggled to remember.

Why did he and I fight?

I couldn't remember.

I remembered shoving him. He wanted to keep

kissing me. And I didn't want him to. I shoved him away from me. Shoved with real anger.

But I couldn't drag up the rest of the scene.

"It makes sense," I murmured in a dull, lifeless voice. "It all makes sense."

I was the only one who lost her memory.

And then I began to draw his face. Every time I started to draw, I sketched Sean's face.

Because of my guilt.

Because my subconscious mind knew that I had murdered him.

"Oh!" I backed away from the bag.

It was too much to bear. I felt about to collapse. My head spun and my knees started to give way.

I heard Adriana's footsteps on the stairs.

And then another horrifying question forced its way into my thoughts: *Does everyone know?*

Does everyone know that I killed him? I wondered, gripped with cold horror.

Does everyone suspect that I was the one?

Is that why they've all acted so strangely around me? Is that why they've been treating me so carefully, so tenderly?

Is that what drove Aaron away?

Because he knew? Because they all know that I'm a *murderer?*

If only I could remember why I killed him. . . .

"Martha—!" Adriana burst into my room. She tried to wrap me in a hug. But I lurched back.

"I know the truth!" I managed to tell her. And then I burst into tears.

Adriana stepped forward and tried again to hug me. This time I didn't move away. "Martha, what are you saying?" she whispered. "Martha, it'll be okay. Really. It'll be okay."

"No, it won't!" I shrieked, pulling away from her. I wiped my cheeks furiously with both hands. "I know the truth!" I insisted. "It won't be okay!"

I could see the confusion on her face. She tugged at her black hair, her dark eyes narrowed on me.

She doesn't know! I realized.

"Look!" I wailed. I dropped down on my knees beside the canvas bag. I pulled it open wide so she could see. "Look!"

Her hands stayed in her hair, tugging tensely as she peered down into the bag. "No," she whispered. "No."

"It's the wire," I told her, even though she already knew. "The leftover wire. And the wire cutters."

"But, Martha—"

"I killed Sean," I said in a low, flat voice. A dead voice. "Here's the proof."

"But, why—?" Adriana demanded, holding on to her hair as if grasping a life preserver.

"I don't know," I answered. "I don't remember. But here's the proof. I killed him. Then I hid the rest of the wire in my bag."

Adriana lowered her eyes to the bag. Then she shut her eyes, and I saw her whole body shudder. "What are you going to do?" she asked.

"Tell Mom and Dad," I replied. "I'm going to

tell Mom and Dad. I guess they'll have to take me to the police."

My words made Adriana jerk back. She fell onto my bed, her hands flying up. "But *why,* Martha? Why did you kill him?"

"I don't remember," I said, shaking my head, trying to force back the tears.

"I saw you two fighting," Adriana remembered. "That night in the cabin. You and Sean went into the back room. I passed by and I saw you arguing. What was it about?"

I shrugged. "I wish I knew. I just can't remember. He kissed me, I think. Or maybe I kissed him. And then we were fighting. And then . . ." My voice trailed off.

I took a deep breath. "I don't know anything for sure. I only know that I'm a murderer."

"No, you're not!"

Another voice invaded my room.

A boy's voice. From the bedroom doorway.

I turned to see Ivan stride in. His black hair disheveled. His dark eyes wild.

"Ivan—!" Adriana cried, jumping up from the bed. "How did you get here? What are you doing here?"

"I followed you," he told his sister. "Martha's parents let me in just before they left."

"But what do you want?" Adriana demanded shrilly. "Martha and I need to talk. We don't need you to—"

He waved his hand hard, a rough, sweeping motion intended to shut her up.

His eyes blazed excitedly as he turned to me.

Has he been drinking? I wondered. Is that why he seems so out of control?

Why did he follow Adriana?

Why did he come here?

"I—I heard what you were saying, Martha," he stammered. His dark eyes burned into mine. "You're wrong. You're not the murderer."

"Huh?" I gasped in shock. "Ivan—what do you mean? Why do you say that?"

He took a deep breath. His chest heaved up and down. Despite the cold of the night, his forehead was drenched with sweat.

"I know you're not the murderer, Martha," he repeated. "Because I am. I murdered Sean."

chapter

23

"**N**o!"

Adriana let out a wild shriek and lunged across the room. She grabbed Ivan by the shoulders and started to shake him wildly.

"No! Why are you saying that? Why?"

He tossed her aside easily. She collided with my dresser, her face twisted in surprise, in fear.

"You're not a murderer!" she screamed at her brother.

"Yes!" he insisted. "I did it, Adriana. I have no choice now. I have to tell the truth. I can't let Martha think she was the one."

Adriana uttered a loud gasp. She opened her mouth to protest, but changed her mind. I saw her shoulders slump, the color drain from her face.

134

Ivan perched on the edge of my desk. His hand nervously brushed the small, black goatee under his chin. He raised his eyes to me. "I couldn't let you think you were the one," he said softly.

"I—I—" I sputtered. I didn't know what to say. I glanced at the canvas bag. It had bared its frightening secret.

And now my life would never be the same.

None of our lives would be the same.

"Why did you kill Sean?" I asked Ivan, softly, almost calmly.

"He found out that I'd stolen a car," Ivan explained. "I stole a car and I wrecked it. I ran away. I wasn't caught."

"I don't believe it," Adriana murmured, shaking her head. She lowered herself to her knees on the floor.

"I made a mistake," Ivan continued. "I told Sean about it. I thought he was my friend. I had to tell someone. I—I was kind of scared. I couldn't keep it to myself. But I never should have told him."

He lowered his head. His dark hair fell over his forehead. He shut his eyes.

"What happened?" I asked softly.

Ivan sighed. "Sean started asking me for money. He said he'd turn me in to the police if I didn't give it to him."

"And did you do it?" Adriana demanded.

Ivan nodded. "What choice did I have? If I got caught stealing that car, I'd be dead meat. My life would be over. So I kept giving Sean the money he asked for. There was just one problem. . . ." His voice trailed off. He rubbed his eyes.

"What problem?" I urged.

"Sean kept asking for more and more. He was never satisfied. I—I—" Ivan's voice broke.

He took a deep breath and started again. "A couple of times I had to steal to get the money for Sean. That's when I knew I had to do something. Something drastic. I couldn't go on paying and paying and paying."

Down on the floor Adriana let out a disgusted groan. But she didn't say anything.

"Did you ever try to talk to Sean?" I demanded. "Did you ever try to reason with him?"

Ivan nodded. "Just before our trip up to the cabins, I tried talking to him. I told him I couldn't pay him any more money."

"And what did he say?" I asked.

A bitter smile crossed Ivan's face. "Sean laughed at me. He said I'd keep paying. Or else he'd go tell my dad." Ivan's smile faded. "That's when I lost it."

"Ivan—" Adriana started.

He waved her quiet again. He kept his eyes on me.

"I found a spool of wire in the back of the hall closet. That's what gave me the idea. When everyone was asleep, I sneaked out and strung the wire between the trees."

Ivan sighed. "I knew Sean would go first. He always had to go first. He had to be the first at everything."

He shook his head sadly. "If only I'd guessed the truth about him when I met him. But he seemed like such a great guy. Everyone liked him. I—I even wanted to *be* like him when I first met him. I didn't know what he was really like—until it was too late."

"So you decided to kill him?" I asked.

"No. No way!" Ivan insisted. "The silver wire—it was real low to the ground. It was just ankle high. I only wanted to knock him down. Maybe hurt him a little."

Ivan let out a low, pained cry. "I know I wasn't thinking clearly. I was out of my head. Crazed. So frightened that Sean really would turn me in. He really would ruin my life."

Ivan climbed to his feet and walked to the window. He leaned on the sill and peered out into the cold, blue night.

"I only wanted to hurt him," he continued. "You know. Scare him. I didn't want to kill him. I don't know what happened. I guess the snow shifted. The wind blew the snow away during the night. So the wire was much higher."

Ivan uttered another cry. "I saw the wire. I saw that it had moved. I saw it—too late. And then I saw Sean's head—and all the blood . . ." His voice trailed off. He swallowed hard.

Adriana jumped up. Her eyes were red. Her features twisted in disgust.

"I'm calling the police," Ivan said, starting across the room to my phone on the desk.

"No—" Adriana protested. She moved to block his way. "Ivan, listen to me—"

"I can't stand the guilt anymore," he said to me. "I can't let you think you did it, Martha. I'm calling the police. I should have done it months ago."

He picked up the phone.

Adriana grabbed it out of his hand. "You idiot!" she screamed. "You stupid idiot!"

Ivan grabbed for the phone. She swiped it out of his reach.

"Give it to me!" Ivan demanded.

"You know you didn't do it!" Adriana shrieked at her brother. "Idiot! You know you didn't kill Sean!"

She pointed at me, her entire body trembling with rage. "Martha killed him! You *know* Martha killed him! She did it! She did!"

chapter

24

*H*er words cut through my heart, stabbed me like a knife.

Why was Adriana accusing me like that?

Did she know the truth? Did she know for sure that I was the murderer?

If so, why was Ivan confessing? Why was Ivan claiming that he did it?

With a furious groan, he grabbed the phone and struggled to wrestle it from her hand.

She spun around, desperate to hold on to it.

"Why are you doing this?" she shrieked at her brother. "Why are you ruining it?"

Ruining it?

What did she mean? I wondered, watching helplessly as they fought. What was she talking about?

"Why are you ruining it?" Adriana cried. "Why are you ruining everything? I worked so hard—and you're going to ruin it!"

She gasped.

She turned to me, her mouth open, her eyes wide.

Her face reddened.

She said too much, I realized. She blurted out more than she meant to.

Before I could react, Ivan grabbed his sister by the shoulders. The phone fell from her hand and clattered to the floor.

"What do you mean?" he demanded. "Explain yourself."

"Ivan, no—!" Adriana protested.

He forced her back against the wall, keeping her arms pinned down at her sides. "Explain. Explain."

For a moment Adriana struggled to free herself. Then I saw the life fade from her eyes. Saw the fight go out of her.

She made no further attempt to get away.

"Ivan, don't ruin it," Adriana pleaded. But I could tell she had given up. Her voice came out in a hoarse whisper, so low I could barely hear her. "Don't ruin it. Don't ruin it," Adriana chanted weakly.

She opened her mouth in a furious cry. "I worked so hard!" she moaned. "And you ruined it. You both ruined it."

"What do you mean?" Ivan demanded, holding

her tightly against the wall. "Are you saying that I *didn't* kill Sean?"

She shook her head sadly. When she raised her eyes to me, I saw cold fury in them. "Sean wasn't supposed to die!" she cried. "It wasn't supposed to be Sean!"

She pointed at me with a trembling finger. "It was supposed to be you, Martha! Why did you ruin everything? You were supposed to die!"

chapter

25

"**A**driana—what are you *saying?*" I cried in shock.

She glared at me, her dark eyes narrowed in fury. She kept pointing, waving her finger at me, as if accusing me, accusing me of a crime.

"Why did you take so long with your ski straps?" she demanded, her voice hoarse now, and ugly. Menacing. "Why did you take so long, Martha?"

"I—I—" I stared back at her open-mouthed. What did she expect me to say?

"You were supposed to go first," she repeated, still pointing, her eyes wild now, wild with fury, brimming with angry tears. "I *told* you to ski first. Because the wire was ready for you."

"Huh?" I gasped, not believing what she was saying.

"I raised the wire." Adriana sneered. "I saw it strung across the slope. I waited till everyone was asleep. Then I went out and raised it. For *you*, Martha. For you!"

She finally lowered her hand. She hugged herself. "Not Sean. Not Sean. Not Sean," she chanted, shaking her head, her dark hair swaying with her.

Ivan took a step back, his eyes dazed. His hands were balled into tight fists, his arms rigid, tense at his sides. "All this time," he murmured weakly, his voice trembling. "All this time I thought I was the murderer. All these months I thought I killed Sean."

I suddenly felt dizzy. Faint. As if Adriana's cruel words had invaded my head. I could almost feel them spinning around in there. I rubbed my temples, trying to force away the dizziness.

"Why—?" I finally managed to choke out. "I don't understand, Adriana. I am your friend. Why? Why did you want to kill me?"

Her dark eyes flared. "Because of Sean!"

"Huh? Sean? What *about* Sean?" I demanded, completely confused.

"I saw Sean first!" Adriana screamed, raising both fists in rage. "Ivan brought him over to the house. I saw him first! Sean and I—there was something special between us. I—I could feel it."

"But, Adriana—" I started.

"Sean didn't know it," she continued, ignoring

143

me. "I don't think he knew it. But I felt it. A special closeness."

An ugly sneer crossed her face. "He wasn't really interested in Laura. She thought he was. Laura always thinks every boy she meets is crazy about her. But Sean wasn't interested in her. *He knew he belonged with me!*"

Adriana screamed these last words at the top of her lungs.

I staggered back a step.

She's crazy, I realized.

Poor Adriana. She's really lost her mind. She isn't making any sense at all.

She had been so stressed out recently. Unable to sleep. Unable to concentrate in school.

But I had no idea. No idea . . .

"Don't stare at me like that!" she shrieked. "I'll scratch your eyes out, Martha. I really will."

Ivan stepped forward. I saw his muscles tense. He was preparing to hold his sister back.

"I—I don't understand," I confessed. "What did I do, Adriana? What did I do to get you so upset?"

"I saw you kissing Sean!" she shrieked. Her chest heaved up and down. She gasped in breath after breath.

"No—!" I cried. "You didn't think—"

"I saw you in the back room of the cabin, Martha. I saw you kissing Sean. And something—something snapped."

She shook her head, her expression bitter. "That's when I knew I had to kill you. You had

Aaron. You had a nice family. Parents who weren't at each other's throats every minute.

"You—you had everything, Martha!" Adriana screamed. "Why did you need Sean too? Why couldn't you leave *something* for me?"

So *that's* what it was all about, I realized finally. It was all a big mistake from beginning to end.

"I didn't *want* Sean to kiss me!" I told Adriana. "He dragged me into the back room because he said he wanted to talk. And then he forced me to kiss him. I pushed him away, Adriana. I wasn't interested in him. I pushed him away and—"

"You *pretended* you were angry!" Adriana accused.

"No—!"

A bitter smile crossed Adriana's face. "I saw you, Martha. I saw you *pretend* to be angry. You pretended to have a fight so that Aaron wouldn't get angry. But you wanted *both* boys! You had to have *both* of them!"

"That's not true!" I screamed. "You're wrong! You were wrong then—and you're wrong now!"

I don't think she heard me. She stared at me with that strange, ugly smile. A smile that wasn't a smile at all.

"The wrong person died," she uttered, lowering her eyes. "Because of you, the wrong person died. I wanted to yell out when he went down the slope. I wanted to stop him. But I was too late. Sean was gone. The only boy I ever cared about. Gone. Because of you."

"Adriana—" Ivan reached out to her. But she stepped away.

"When you lost your memory," she continued, raising her eyes to me. "When you lost your memory, I knew it was my chance to cover up my crime."

I gasped. "What do you mean?"

"I bought some wire and hid it in the bottom of your bag," Adriana confessed. "Then, after my visits to the doctor, I hypnotized you."

"Huh? You *what?*" I shrieked, raising my hands to the sides of my face, gaping at her in disbelief.

I saw Ivan gasp too.

"Dr. Corben was such a good teacher. And I learned so quickly," Adriana continued, her strange smile returning. "I gave you hypnotic suggestions, Martha. To keep you from remembering. I hypnotized you to keep you from remembering the truth."

"I don't believe it," I murmured, my hands still pressing against my cheeks. "And you left that message, that ugly phone message."

"I wanted you to *feel* guilty," Adriana said. "I wanted you to *feel* deep down that you were the murderer." The strange smile faded slowly.

"But then you started to remember," she murmured, lowering her eyes. "Then you started drawing Sean's face over and over. That was your memory, trying to force its way back. That was your subconscious mind, guiding your hand."

She scowled at me, narrowing her eyes coldly. "I

146

kept hypnotizing you. Kept giving you hypnotic suggestions. Tried to push your memories back. But . . . but . . ."

Adriana opened her mouth and let out a cry, a horrifying cry of pain and anger.

"Sean died because of you, Martha. I can't let you go on living your perfect life as if nothing happened!"

Before I could move, Adriana dived to the floor.

She pulled the coiled-up silver wire from the bag.

Ivan moved to stop her. He lunged toward his sister.

She spun quickly. Raised a knee.

Caught him in the pit of the stomach.

He groaned. His eyes bulged in surprise. In pain.

He crumbled to the floor.

"Adriana—no!" I tried to shout, but my voice came out in a hoarse croak.

I started to back away.

Too late.

Adriana grabbed me. Grabbed me roughly.

Whirled me around.

I saw the cold hatred in her eyes.

And before I could cry out, she had the silver wire around my throat.

And pulled it tight.

I felt it cut into my skin.

I couldn't breathe.

I couldn't breathe at all.

chapter
26

*T*he wire cut into my throat.

Adriana pulled the wire tighter. Tighter.

I raised my hands. Tried to grab her.

But I could feel my strength flowing away. Emptying out. My life emptying out.

I made another weak grab for Adriana.

Staggered forward.

I backed her into the desk. We both crashed hard against it, sending papers flying all over.

I twisted around. Tried to pull away.

But I couldn't escape.

Ivan? Where was Ivan?

Still doubled over on the floor.

"Aaaaach." A final choking gasp escaped my throat.

I felt so weak. So weak and frightened.

No breath.

No breath left.

I shut my eyes.

Saw only white. Such a clean, pure white.

"Unh unh unnnnh."

What was that strange sound?

"Unnnnh. Unnnh."

The sound of me dying?

No. Breathing.

I was breathing again. Sucking in breath after breath.

"Unnnnh. Unnnnh." Breathing noisily.

The silver cord had loosened. Enough so that I could breathe.

I opened my eyes.

What had happened to Adriana? Why had she stopped strangling me? Why had she stopped? Why was I still alive?

I struggled to focus. The bright, pure white faded so slowly . . . slowly.

I sucked in another chestful of air.

Adriana?

She was staring down at the desktop. She had let go of the silver cord.

She stared at the desktop, her hands at her sides.

I blinked the pure white away. I had to see what she was staring at.

I finally focused. And saw the face.

My drawing of Sean's face. The drawing had tumbled out of the pad.

Adriana stared at the face as if hypnotized.

"Adriana—?"

She didn't move. Didn't blink. Didn't *breathe*.

She stared at my drawing. Stared at Sean. And he appeared to stare back at her.

They stared at each other, Adriana and the dead boy, the boy she had loved.

Ivan stepped up behind her and removed the wire from her hand. He grabbed her wrists and held her in place.

But she didn't move.

"Call for help," Ivan said softly.

I turned away, rubbing my throat. I will, I thought. I'll call the police. I knew they would get help for Adriana.

I knew I was okay now. Knew we were all okay. Knew the nightmare was over.

I slumped into Ivan's arms. We held each other, so tightly.

And still Adriana didn't move.

She stared unblinking, hypnotized by the face.

The face that had puzzled me, upset me— horrified me for so long.

The face that had saved my life.

About the Author

"Where do you get your ideas?"

That's the question that R. L. Stine is asked most often. "I don't know where my ideas come from," he says. "But I do know that I have a lot more scary stories in my mind that I can't wait to write."

So far, he has written over fifty mysteries and thrillers for young people, all of them bestsellers.

Bob grew up in Columbus, Ohio. Today he lives in an apartment near Central Park in New York City with his wife, Jane, and fifteen-year-old son, Matt.

THE NIGHTMARES NEVER END . . . WHEN YOU VISIT

Next . . .
SECRET ADMIRER
(Coming in mid-February 1996)

Selena is on top of the world. Everyone at Shadyside High can see that she's going to be a famous actress someday. Everyone admires her. But someone admires her too much.

When Selena starts receiving bouquets of dead flowers from a person called "The Sun," she treats them as a joke. But The Sun makes it clear that this is no laughing matter. First, Selena's understudy is injured in a suspicious "accident." Then a speeding car nearly kills Selena herself.

Anonymous notes tell her that "The Sun" is responsible.

Now Selena's number-one fan has become her number-one nightmare.